NIGHT MANOEUVRES

The garden was damp, with clammy spiders' webs that fell across their faces. A feral cat fled over an avalanche of loose rubbish into deep shadow. Beamish touched Mosley's sleeve.

"There's someone in the house."

There was the faint movement of a source of light in one of the upstairs rooms.

"I'll stay here," Mosley said. "You go round to the front."

Left alone, Mosley sat down on a pile of rubble, patient and motionless. An owl hooted in one of the trees in the Park. The cat, taking courage, stalked back to its original ambush. A shoot of overgrown rambler tapped arrhythmically against a window pane. There was no further sign of movement in the house. Mosley's breathing was slow, deep, and regular. Then somewhere in the night a woman screamed. It was in the front of the house. Mosley did not stir. He was happy to leave this to Beamish.

Bantam offers the finest in classic and modern British murder mysteries.
Ask your bookseller for the books you have missed.

Agatha Christie

Death on the Nile
A Holiday for Murder
The Mousetrap and Other Plays
The Mysterious Affair at Styles
Poirot Investigates
Postern of Fate
The Secret Adversary
The Seven Dials Mystery
Sleeping Murder

Dorothy Simpson

Last Seen Alive
The Night She Died
Puppet for a Corpse
Six Feet Under
Close Her Eyes
Coming Soon: Element of Doubt

Sheila Radley

The Chief Inspector's Daughter
Death in the Morning
Fate Worse Than Death
Who Saw Him Die?

Elizabeth George

A Great Deliverance

Colin Dexter

Last Bus to Woodstock
The Riddle of the Third Mile
The Silent World of Nicholas Quinn
Service of All the Dead
The Dead of Jericho
The Secret of Annexe 3
Coming Soon: Last Seen Wearing

John Greenwood

The Mind of Mr. Mosley
The Missing Mr. Mosley
Mosley by Moonlight
Murder, Mr. Mosley
Mists Over Mosley
What, Me, Mr. Mosley?

Ruth Rendell

A Dark-Adapted Eye
  (writing as Barbara Vine)
A Fatal Inversion
  (writing as Barbara Vine)

Marian Babson

Death in Fashion
Reel Murder
Murder, Murder Little Star
Murder on a Mystery Tour

Christianna Brand

Suddenly at His Residence
Heads You Lose

Dorothy Cannell

The Widows Club
Coming Soon: Down the Garden Path

Michael Dibdin

Ratking

What, Me, Mr. Mosley?

John Greenwood

BANTAM BOOKS
TORONTO · NEW YORK · LONDON · SYDNEY · AUCKLAND

WHAT, ME, MR. MOSLEY?

A Bantam Book / published by arrangement with
Walker Publishing Company, Inc.

PRINTING HISTORY
Walker edition published February 1988
Bantam edition / February 1989

ISBN 0-553-27715-4

Published simultaneously in the United States and Canada

Bantam Books are published by Bantam Books, a division of Bantam Doubleday
Dell Publishing Group, Inc. Its trademark, consisting of the words "Bantam Books"
and the portrayal of a rooster, is Registered in U.S. Patent and Trademark Office
and in other countries. Marca Registrada. Bantam Books, 666 Fifth Avenue, New
York, New York 10103.

PRINTED IN THE UNITED STATES OF AMERICA

KR   0 9 8 7 6 5 4 3 2 1

One

Bagshawe Broome: an 1860s town hall whose solid neo-gothic furbelows proclaim the venerability of the borough fathers of the day. A century and a quarter later it is a grimy pile, though it is at least three decades since soot has been dispersed from any of the town's mill chimneys. Indeed, all but one of those chimneys has by now been caused to bite its own dust, the exception being Bowland's, up Mere Brow, which, although visibly idle and unsafe, has enjoyed several stays of execution, thanks to the efforts of the litigious members of the BIAS, the Bagshawe Industrial Archaeology Society, to have a preservation order slapped on to it.

Bagshawe Broome: a Saturday in October. A three-ton lorry, loaded with ironmongers' sundries, is endeavouring to retract over the cobbles between market stalls, to the voluble and profane distress of the driver of a greengrocer's van who has been trying for the last ten minutes to reverse out. Housewives are compelled to reverse their shoulders into piles of Common Market apples and a small child on a tricycle runs over the foot of the deputy mayoress. A uniformed constable, scenting a situation, disappears up an alley between the Midland Bank and The Cheapest Discount Stores in the North-West, where there is no situation.

But another member of the same force is in the thick of the trading. A solid little man with his greatcoat flapping open, a black homburg jammed tightly and evenly on his head, is gazing at a stall from behind a band of enthusiastic pickers-over of the goods on offer.

1

Two things may be giving him food for thought. One is the merchandise itself, which includes a single (left-footed) dancing shoe, possibly abandoned by a Cinderella in some *Palais de Danse* of the late 1920s; a wooden smoothing plane, perfectly usable if its purchaser can find a wedge and a blade to fit it; a silver-plated Edwardian writing-stand, complete but for one of its inkwells; and a small, heavily gilt-framed oil-painting, so patinaed with a century's escape of smoke from a coal-fire that it has acquired a certain super-ficially Rembrandtesque quality.

Dickie Holgate, General Dealer, a young, charismatically energetic, cheerfully bantering man in shirt sleeves is in no way apologetic for any defects in his stock-in-trade. *As Found* has become the commercial motto of his stall. Every *emptor* speculates under this perpetual *caveat*, and the second thing that may possibly have impressed Detective-Inspector Mosley is the eager acquisitiveness of Bagshawe. A middle-aged woman, who looks affluent enough to toast by electricity, has just given fifty pence for a metal toasting fork. Manufactured between the wars, its prongs are bent and stained, as if it has been used for unclogging something. A man is tendering two pound coins for a Number Two Brownie box camera that looks as if it has spent some years under a pile of rotting leaves. And two women are about to fall out over an ebonite letter-opener with a furry handle fashioned like a goat's foot.

There is reason behind Bagshawe's herd desire to invest in wartime civilian respirators, cockle-shell-encrusted cameos of blue skies over Morecambe, pre-steam-age flat-irons and walking-sticks with gun-metal knobs. Three months ago television's Antiques Road Show set up shop in Bradcaster Corn Exchange. Staid couples from as far afield as Hadley Dale and Lower Pattershaw travelled to the city clutching brown paper parcels. An OAP from Upper Crud-shaw had a blue and white Lowestoft porringer, now valued by the experts at £2,000, from which a dynasty of cats had been lapping up meanly watered milk for the last forty-five years. An elderly brother-and-sister from Bradburn brought in an elegantly French eighteenth-century bread hutch, bought two world wars ago by their great-uncle for half a

2

crown at an auction in Cleckheaton. They were now advised to insure it for four figures. A Martin Brothers mask jug, which had been catching drips under a leaky roof up Lanthorn Hill, was reserved for special exhibition at the end of the programme: Jug of the Match.

The programme had given Bagshawe Broome food for thought. For years, as elderly relatives had departed, Bagshawe Broome had been disposing, sometimes with secretive ingenuity, of just such trifles as were now changing hands at stratospheric figures. Systematically they began to reacquire such similar objects as they could find on sale at *As Found* valuation. In every market place from Rawtenstall to Settle there was now a stall run by men like Dickie Holgate, some of them palpably more honest than others, who were keeping potential treasures in circulation at keenly competitive prices.

And it seemed that even Inspector Mosley was in the field for the appreciation of once-despised junk. He positively elbowed his way to the counter's edge and put his hand on a Victorian leather correspondence-case for which a woman in a hand-knitted tam o'shanter was just reaching out. She looked at him murderously and he removed himself rapidly to another sector of the display, where he picked up a George III butter-knife. Then he went for the incomplete inkstand, whose tarnished silver plaque bore the engraved initials WFH.

Dickie Holgate, who considered himself on excellent terms with the Inspector, watched his acquisitive keenness with some amusement.

'That'll be eleven pounds altogether, Mr Mosley.'

'You'll have to be satisfied with a receipt,' Mosley said.

Dickie laughed.

'Well, if the credit of the law isn't sound, I don't know what is.'

Mosley did not answer. He looked at the stall-holder with the sort of intensity that froze his smile.

'I won't hang about now. I'll come back and see you before you pack up.'

He hurried away, as if he did not want to interfere with the trade: in the presence of their most unpredictable policeman, there was a noticeable tendency of people to retreat a few yards. He did not go far, but sat down on an empty box at the end of Jimmy Brigg's fruit-stall and came back with three official slips that he handed to Holgate. He was about to turn away again, but Holgate did not want to be kept in suspense.

'You're not worried about those bits of things, are you, Mr Mosley?'

'I'm worried about you,' Mosley said, almost ventriloquially, as if he did not want to be heard by any of the curiously watching customers.

'What, me, Mr Mosley? I can tell you where I got these. House clearance. Garth. Bowland Avenue. Tim Fawcett, the auctioneer, put it my way.'

'I'll come and have a word with you before you've packed up.'

Two

Garth, Bowland Avenue: Henry Burgess. Mosley had known him, as indeed had anyone else who had at any time strolled the streets of Bagshawe Broome.

Bowland Avenue was an unmade-up cul-de-sac leading out of the middle of Dickinson Road. Dickinson Road, which lay between the town centre and its outer ring of newer houses, was a haven of substantial red-brick Victorian villas that at the zenith of Bagshawe Broome's prosperity had been the preserve of mill-owners, senior professional men and the type of negotiant who commuted daily to Bradcaster or Manchester. Bowland Avenue served a single house, set back and apart from the autocratic residences of Dickinson Road as if it disdained them. It was vaster than any of them and set in jealously enclosed grounds that dwarfed them all – as indeed had done its founder-resident, the Bowland of Bowland's, whose now smokeless and perilous chimney the die-hards of BIAS still wished to preserve. When Bowland died in the early 1920s, his house was bought by Henry Burgess – to be more exact, by Henry Burgess's newly acquired wife – and there were few in Bagshawe Broome now who could remember anyone but Henry Burgess living at Garth.

Mosley knew Henry Burgess by reputation, and indulged in polite small-talk with him on several occasions: Henry Burgess was prepared to accede to polite small-talk with anyone whom he had seen about for a minimum of twenty years, or for whom he had ever cashed a cheque at the

5

Midland Bank. Mosley also knew that Burgess had died a few weeks ago, of natural and not unexpected causes, on the threshold of his ninety-fourth year. Burgess was a former bank clerk, whose forty-odd years of service had not elevated him beyond cashier, and who had retired before computers and credit cards. True, he had come in a little later than Dickensian hand-ruled ledgers, but he carried the look of those days about with him. It was three decades since Henry Burgess had last double-counted a stack of notes, so there was no one in Bagshawe under the age of fifty who could picture him even doing that. It was sixty-three years since he had become a widower, so no one in the town could truthfully remember his wife. It was still said that he had been inconsolably grieved by his bereavement, and that that accounted for his inaccessibility and lack of friends. In fact for the last twenty years, most of those who might have been his friends were themselves already dead.

The wife of whom present-day Bagshawe could speak only notionally had brought significant funds to their union: hence Garth, which even at the Midland Bank was said to be absurdly above his station. But he continued to live there, alone, for more than sixty less-than-glorious years and had managed the house without help until after his seventieth birthday, when the awe-inspiring Mrs Toplady had started coming in to do for him. That arrangement had finished abruptly about two years ago and no account of the supposed breach had been released by either side. There was speculation by the curious, and rather more by those with a taste for the grotesque, but no one really believed the stories that were current for a time. It was generally thought – not that anyone cared – that what had happened was simply a clash of inflexible temperaments. Various welfare workers had inserted toes round Henry Burgess's front door, but he had resisted all attempts to get a helpful footing into his regime. At one time his GP bullied him into suffering meals on wheels to be delivered to him twice a week, but he complained querulously about the quality of the food and was eventually so rude to a voluntary helper that the team refused to enter his premises again.

He was a dark-suited, lantern-cheeked man with a jaw

like a snow-plough. He belonged to a distant past and his gait and bearing made it clear that he did not want things otherwise. Until he was eighty he had had acquaintances whom he was prepared tacitly to tolerate, and one evening a week he would make his slow way across to Bagshawe Broome's grossly misnamed Literary Club to play a few hands of nasty-tempered bridge, the cards mattering to him more than did anyone at the table. For many years his midday meal was a sandwich or pie from Bert Hardcastle's kiosk, which he ate standing in a corner of the Market Place, only on the foulest of days taking the food home. It was at times like that that a few accepted men like Mosley could sometimes draw him into conversation, but never on topics deeper than the weather or the insane pronouncements of some politician to the left of ultra-conservative.

Whenever he had to eat in Bagshawe, Mosley was also a loyal customer of Bert Hardcastle's. Bert's sandwiches contained a prodigious quantity of ham, cheese or cold roast beef, and housewives often took them home to serve their contents as the major item of their husbands' supper. Bert argued that he made swingeing profits on his cups of tea, and that the food he sold was a loss-leader to get clients to his counter. But there were many who believed that no business could stand such a loss and that Hardcastle was subsidizing his sandwiches to gain himself an improbable reputation: there are men in Mosley's country who vie with each other in that kind of eccentricity.

Mosley was still clutching the bric-a-brac he had requisitioned from Dickie Holgate as he stood eating a sandwich nearly an inch and a half thick outside Bert Hardcastle's kiosk. Alex Balmforth, retired manager of one of Bagshawe's other banks, and an erstwhile younger member of Burgess's bridge school, came up for bread and cheese.

'Old Henry's no longer with us, then?'

'It hardly came as a surprise, you know,' Balmforth said. 'You could see the old man failing, these last few months.'

'Slowing down, you mean?'

'He could hardly have slowed down without actually stalling. No. I mean he was crumbling mentally. He was more distant, more deeply entrenched in his own world – I

7

know that hardly seems possible. Yet the last time I spoke to him he suddenly remembered how I once over-called when I was partnering him, all of fifteen years ago. He still took it as an indication of my mental inadequacy.'

Then Mosley ran into Arthur Murgatroyd, traffic warden, who had earned a personal relationship with Henry Burgess by pulling him back from a close encounter with an articulated lorry. Old Henry had never forgotten him for interfering.

'He didn't like me drawing attention to his carelessness in public, thought I was trying to show him up. Of course, the old man hadn't been himself for some time.'

'Healthwise, you mean?'

'Not only that – though I suppose his whole system was packing up, really. He wasn't entirely with it any more. Only natural, I suppose we've got to say: senile whatever-they-call-it. He was preoccupied, looking into outer space. Yet in some respects he was still on the ball. You could set your watch by him shuffling up to Bert's for his lunch, coming out for his evening paper, turning up for the Friday night pint he always treated himself to in the Lansdowne.'

'He liked his pint still, then?'

'Once a week. I wouldn't go so far as to say he liked it. He never looked as if he was enjoying it, but apparently it had started with one or two of the other clerks from the Midland in the thirties, and he had always kept it up. Habits died hard with old Henry.'

Mosley dropped in at the Lansdowne Arms, the hours being extended for market day.

'Came once a week. Stayed half an hour. Talked to no one. Once or twice the youngsters tried to pull his leg, but they gave it up when he didn't want to know them.'

The landlord of the Lansdowne got up an annual Christmas party for old-age pensioners – he had a collecting-box on the counter all the year round. But he had never been able to persuade Henry Burgess to come. The old man had seemed to resent the offer as an intrusion.

'Well, last year we started delivering goodies to those who were house-bound, and some of the chaps tried taking a parcel to Henry. But if they hadn't looked smart with their

8

feet and elbows, they wouldn't have got past his front door.'

The landlord was called to serve a round in another bar. When he came back, he was still pulling the same face he had been pulling when he left.

'Mickey Darwent and Harold Hawthorn were the two who went. You ought to have heard what they had to say about it. They couldn't make head or tail of what was going on. How well do you know that neighbourhood, Mr Mosley?'

'Not down to the last stick and cranny.'

'It's not a stone's throw from the centre of town, but when he built that house old Bowland took care there weren't going to be any Peeping Toms. There were fields at the back, and it was not till after the Second World War that the council got their thieving hands on the land at the ratepayers' expense and turned it into Westwood Park. So really, it isn't all that much different now. As for Henry Burgess's back garden – the shrubs haven't been cut back for so long, they're more like trees. And it's the same at the front: you can hardly see the house from the gate. And when Mickey and Harold had shut the gate behind them, they could hardly believe their ears. There was pop music blaring out full pelt. Hard rock, so bloody loud they wondered if old man Burgess had gone stone deaf. It sounded as if he was giving a party for half the punks and rockers in the district.'

The landlord was a man who did not take his story-telling lightly. His eyeballs threatened to burst with the effort of putting this one over.

'But when they pulled the bell – it was one of those that works on a rusty old wire – all this racket suddenly stopped.'

'There may not be anything all that wonderful about that,' Mosley said. 'You can produce silence at the turn of a knob. Maybe he'd gone out of the room and hadn't realized what programme he'd switched on.'

'That's what I tried to tell them. But Mickey and Harold said it was weird. Henry Burgess lived mostly in his kitchen, didn't really use any of his other rooms. We know that, because of what Primrose Toplady has told people up and down. I don't think there's a soul in Bagshawe Broome who's ever seen the inside of one of his other rooms. And come to that, there's not many ever been in his kitchen – only the plumber, when he's had a winter burst, and the men who read the meters. Henry Burgess always did for himself, till Mrs Toplady started going in, and Mickey and Harold said that the kitchen was pretty run-down. There'd been no interior decoration for years. He'd sat on his cushions so long that he'd flattened them.'

It was perhaps a pity that some impresario had not talent-spotted the landlord as an international mime artiste. The face he was now wearing must be draining him of nervous energy.

'Old Henry said he didn't want the parcel, but they left it with him. They could see it was Scrooge all over again. He didn't want reminding it was Christmas.'

Mosley came to the end of his modest half-pint of mild and made it clear that he wanted no more.

'Old Henry didn't exactly kick them out. He didn't have to – they were glad enough to go. The place got on a man's wheel. But then a funny thing happened. They hadn't got halfway across the front garden, when the racket in the house started up again: progressive rock, the volume turned up so high that the radio must have been dancing on the table.'

'Happen he'd got the same wavelength as before.'

'If he had, it was what he wanted. He didn't turn it off this time. They could hear the bloody noise behind them until they were well out in Dickinson Road.'

The landlord was called elsewhere and Mosley left the pub. He made his way to Bowland Avenue, not approaching from the Dickinson Road angle, but going round through Westwood Park, where he was seen by quite a number of people who would have liked to pass the time of day with him. But Mosley did not see any of them. He seemed entirely wrapped up in himself, totally oblivious of those about him. He struck out diagonally across the grass to the hedge at the bottom of Henry Burgess's garden – an enormous growth, now at least eight feet high, that had not been trimmed for years, and would have to be tackled by its new owner from a plank between tall ladders. Two senior citizens, sitting on a bench some fifty yards from him, both saw him there, gazing into its depths, as if there was some secret that he was willing the vegetation to give up. Then he walked the length of that hedge, once in either direction. Seconds later, he was no longer there, and his disappearance became that evening's main talking point in Bagshawe. The legend went the rounds that he had plunged through the privet like a Churchill tank through a bed of nettles.

Three

Desmond Lummis (A Levels: Grade C Eng Lit, Grade D Economics, Failed History) was one of Bagshawe Broome's generation of rising strengths who did not know Mosley. In sole charge of Fawcett and Foster's estate agency on the key afternoon of the week, Lummis was supercilious with the confidence of his two years' experience.

'Really, Inspector – I would have expected an officer of your standing to know better than to ask that sort of question. I cannot discuss a client's confidential business.'

Mosley's response was a deflating show of patience.

'You are quite right to take that attitude.'

But the young man, if deflatable, was not deflated. He obviously regarded Mosley's soft tongue as a smoke signal of defeat, whereas in the eyes of the initiated it was a warning sign. But at that moment Tim Fawcett came in.

Timothy John Fawcett was a sleepy man whose eyelids drooped over dark pupils that did not by the remotest glint promise hidden life within. Young people of the executive class, when putting their houses on Bagshawe Broome's speculative estates on the market, tended to avoid Fawcett and Foster, and in this they were mistaken, for without ever appearing to exert himself, Tim Fawcett was always magically half a length ahead of his competitors. Marginal loss of business through a fallacious reputation did not worry him. The bulk of his income came from the valuation and transfer of licensed premises and he had sleepily cornered sixty per cent of the business in this field over four northern counties.

'Your young man was just about to tell me about Henry Burgess,' Mosley said with gentle malevolence.

'Oh, yes?'

Fawcett closed his eyes for so long that some would-be conversationalists would have resigned. But Mosley waited some fifteen respectful seconds, then spoke again.

'Not a big spender, old Henry. Quite a lot of nice pieces in the house, I should imagine, especially from his wife's side. And there are hardly likely to be any charges on the property. Who gets the lion's share? The Midland Bank Down-and-out Staff Association?'

'A niece. Nancy Batham. Married to a quantity surveyor in South Staffs. Nice girl. Well, not far off the forty mark.'

'No other beneficiaries?'

'Two younger brothers, who don't feature in the will.'

'Perhaps she had cultivated the old man?'

'She came over every two or three years.'

'And there's stuff worth having – apart from a hundred thousand quids' worth of house and grounds?'

'There's a dressing-table that's undoubtedly Sheraton, a cabinet of Derby porcelain that's going to be called important, probably pre-Duesbury, any number of collectable bits and pieces. Bedroom furniture that will appeal to some: wardrobes and chests of drawers modelled on St Pancras Station.'

'And obviously any amount of smaller stuff?'

'That doesn't bother me. I run an auction room, not a sweet-shop. Mrs Batham has earmarked what she wants, and she's no magpie. I've sold the trivia as a job lot to a house clearance man.'

'Dickie Holgate.'

Fawcett went into one of his longer blinks.

'Has he had enough experience?' Mosley asked.

'He's getting it.'

'You deal with him a lot?'

'More and more. He's good. Gets on with it. Leaves the place clean. Burns the rubbish. Can be trusted alone in a room. Doesn't argue over a fair offer.'

'And doubtless lives in hope of finding a fortune in the false bottom of a drawer?'

'A reliable dealer is worth keeping sweet. I make a point of leaving him a few bits and bobs that are worth having.'

'Like bits and bobs with the initials WFH on them?'

'I noticed a few of those about the house. I don't know who WFH was.'

'I do.'

Fawcett's eyelids fell. He did not ask. Mosley did not tell him.

'Is there an inventory?'

'Of the small stuff? We would be at it for ever. All I want is to get it out of the way.'

'So you've given Dickie Holgate a deadline?'

'End of the month.'

Mosley took his leave. In the outer office Desmond Lummis wished him good afternoon as if he were a valued old friend.

Mosley went back to the market, approaching the stalls from behind. There was now a bleak wooden emptiness about most of them. Yellowing cabbage leaves clung obstinately to the cobbles, defying the assault of bass brooms. There was a suggestion in the air that at least one consignment of fish was nearing the end of its commercial viability. Dickie Holgate had by now packed most of his remnants into tea-chests and cardboard cartons. He waved cheerily to Mosley. Mosley stood impassively to one side, saying and doing nothing to hurry him. A young woman came up breathlessly, hugging a stack of tattered Mills and Boon paperbacks.

'Am I too late?'

Holgate showed her in which box he had stowed away his secondhand romances. She began to lift handfuls of them out.

Holgate took her money, tidied up after her.

'She reads ten a week,' he told Mosley. 'They get them for half price if they bring their old ones back.'

Mosley did not appear interested.

'I want us to go together to Garth.'

Holgate drove them there in his van, working hard to get Mosley to talk about something, anything. Mosley looked

14

out of the window, apparently hell-bent on not committing himself to the frailest thread of amiability.

'You're treating me as if I were a criminal,' Holgate said.

'I shall if you are one.'

'Thanks.'

Holgate parked in Bowland Avenue, held open the garden gate for Mosley to precede him. It hung on one hinge that was not going to last much longer. The garden had not been managed for years. Burgess had even given up having the lawn cut, and an autumn that had so far been slow to bite had encouraged this year's grass to go on growing. Here and there one could trace a history of beds and herbaceous borders. A few blue bells of campanula peeped in spidery fashion from behind straggling greenery. Marigolds had spread. Golden rod had proliferated like a nodding forest. Nettles stood seven feet high.

Holgate had a key and let them in. There were a few items of junk mail underfoot: American Express were still trying to sell Henry Burgess a charge card.

'I didn't know they were valid where he's gone,' Holgate said.

Mosley did not pick up the pleasantry. They went together into the large room to the left of the entrance hall. It must once have been the dining-room – in Henry Burgess's wife's day – though it was an inconsiderately long way from the kitchen. There was a sweet fungoid smell in the air.

'Whoever buys this is going to keep Rentokil in business,' Dickie Holgate said.

Mosley did not answer, but stood looking suggestively at the array of objects on the central table: a cased, silver-backed brush and comb set, an Edwardian chain purse, a patent oil-fuelled reading lamp, a hip flask, a lady's umbrella with a tortoiseshell handle, two napkin rings in a case.

'You're using this as a store room, are you?' Mosley asked.

'I've not really started systematically on the place. Next week. I just took one or two things to fill gaps on this morning's stall.'

Holgate looked at the collection on the table with sudden concentration.

15

'Mr Mosley – some things are missing.'

Mosley waited unexcitedly to be told. There were, in fact, empty spaces on the table.

'Things have gone since I was last here, last night. There was a massive antique boxed set of geometrical instruments. A buff would pay no end for that. There was a cut glass celery holder, set in silver. There was a carriage clock. Somebody has been here, Mr Mosley.'

'I know. I have.'

'*You* have?'

'This afternoon.'

'Isn't that pushing your rights a bit, Mr Mosley?'

'I dare say. I don't expect anything much to come of it.'

'So where are those things – the carriage clock, the celery jar – ?'

'Safe. You shall have all the proper documentation. But let's not do it in penny numbers. Let's make one job of it when we're through with the lot, shall we?'

'Would you mind telling me what this is about, Mr Mosley?'

'Don't you ever read the stolen property lists that we send out?'

'There's such a lot of stuff. I get behind.'

'You shouldn't. We don't put them out for fun. Did you notice any common feature about those articles that I've impounded?'

Dickie Holgate thought.

'Weren't there initials on them – the writing-case, the clock, even the celery glass?'

'What initials?'

Holgate did not remember at once, but they came to him.

'WFH?'

'Who's WFH?'

'How the hell should I know?'

'Stolen property, Mr Holgate. All those things were missing after a break-in at Lytham St Anne's two years ago – a summer residence shut up for the winter.'

'So how can they have got into Henry Burgess's hands?'

'Perhaps they didn't.'

'I don't know what I'm supposed to read into that.'

16

'Perhaps they didn't get here until after Mr Burgess's sad demise.'

'I don't see what you're getting at.'

'If a man had dubious property to dispose of, house clearance would be a very handy way to claim he had come by it.'

Holgate digested this.

'Meaning me, Mr Mosley?'

Mosley looked wildly behind himself and under the table. He opened a corner cupboard and stuck his head into it.

I don't think we have company, have we?'

'Mr Mosley – '

'Dickie – I had a quiet little word with you when you were first setting up in business. Do you remember what I said?'

'A little fireside chat about honesty.'

'I told you, Dickie, that in the walk of life that you've elected for, it's not easy to be honest. You've got to be so honest that it's your honesty men talk about. You've got to start that way – and stay so. You've got to wear your honesty on both sleeves. Once you lose your name for honesty, you'll never get it back.'

'I do my little best, Mr Mosley.'

Then suddenly he came near to losing his temper.

'Mr Mosley, I find it offensive that you should be treating me as some sort of suspect.'

And he remembered something else.

'And if it's proof you want, when Tim Fawcett first brought me here to show me round, I picked up that carriage clock, and I said to him, "I wonder who WFH was." And he said, "Oh, some dim and distant heirloom-dispenser on one side or other of the Burgess marriage." I bet he'll remember saying that.'

'Or he'll have inconveniently forgotten. I'll ask him next time I see him. Let's take a little walk round the house.'

There was discoloration of the walls. Cables of cobweb hung where Tim Fawcett had had some of the more massive pieces removed to his saleroom. Like so many houses of this period, this one had been designed as a public proclamation of prosperity, rather than for the convenience of any of

17

those who had to live or work in it. The great rooms must have been mercilessly cold, and even before the trees outside had matured, they must have been dark. Now that the foliage had luxuriated at random, there was a gloom about the place that seemed to reflect Henry Burgess's inconsolable and peevish misery. And, of course, many of the rooms had not been entered for years.

'Which was old Henry's bedroom, do you know?'

'This one,' Dickie Holgate said.

It was one of the smaller ones, as if the old man had moved into it as a monastic penance. It was probably as a young man that he had made that choice. The bed was a single one of vintage hospital ward pattern. The mattress was one of the things that Dickie Holgate would be throwing on to his terminal bonfire. There were medicines on the stained cane table beside the bed: nothing extraordinary – prescriptions against the coughs and discomforts of old age. The room seemed still to smell of Henry Burgess: of his urine, his old man's breath, his dandruff and his desquamating armpits. Mosley did not spend long in there, but for some reason not obvious to Holgate he seemed to want to linger in one of the other rooms. It was a spacious double room at the back of the house – what must surely have been the matrimonial bedroom was at the front, and had presumably been derelict since Burgess's wife's death. In this guestroom, Mosley looked long and thoughtfully out of the window.

The back garden was even more a wilderness than the front one. The remains of a row of rotting canes were still stuck in the ground, as if someone had grown runner beans here fifteen years ago. The handles of a very old, very rusty and very basic mower were just about visible in a tangle of woody nightshade and fat hen. Honeysuckle had overreached the summit of a dying apple tree and bindweed had taken possession of the pole that brought in the overhead electricity mains.

Mosley turned and gave his attention to the interior of the room. He ran a finger along the dust on the window-ledge and cursorily examined what he retrieved. Then he stooped, picked up something tiny, dropped it into the palm of his hand and examined it close to the light from the window. Then he brought it over, and showed it to Holgate.

'What do you reckon this is?'

Holgate looked.

'Easy. It's the stylus from a stereogram.'

'Can you think of any reason why Henry Burgess should be changing the stylus of a stereogram in a bedroom that he never used?'

'Bit of a facer, that one.'

'Perhaps his niece brought one with her when she stayed here?'

Mosley put the stylus away in his wallet and let Dickie Holgate drive away alone. He spent a little more time looking up and down inside the house, then walked back along Dickinson Road, stopping at the first telephone kiosk he encountered. From here he rang Tim Fawcett at his number.

'Tim – has Dickie Holgate been in touch with you since I was talking to you in your office?'

'No.'

'He will be. He'll be asking if you remember him asking you about the initials WFH. And you're supposed to have said something about an ancestor of Henry Burgess or his wife.'

'I did say something along those lines.'

'I want you to deny it – or at least to make out that you don't remember the question coming up.'

'If you want me to.'

'This is important, Tim.'

'I'll take your word for it.'

Mosley hung up. Fawcett had not asked him why. He had sounded lethargic and uninterested as if he were about to drop off with the receiver at his ear.

'What,' the assistant chief constable asked Detective-Superintendent Tom Grimshaw, 'is Mosley up to nowadays? We seem to hear nothing of him.'

'And are we complaining on that score?'

'No – but it is the same syndrome as a quiet child.'

'I know what you mean. In fact, only yesterday I was reflecting that about the only serious detection I do these days is trying to interpret the visible and outward signs of Mosley's activities. He seems at the moment to be conducting himself as an orthodox detective.'

'I find that worrying. Do you think he is sickening for something?'

'I think he's behaving himself for a purpose. My belief is that he's about to ask a favour.'

'Ask a favour? Mosley?'

'Yes. I think he's about to ask if Beamish can be permanently seconded to him. He's already dropped a hint or two.'

'A good idea.'

'It's a terrible idea. I shall resist it with every argument I can muster. It would be the ruin of Beamish. It would simply make another Mosley of him.'

Four

Stately as a galleon –

Anyone familiar with Joyce Grenfell's song must surely have found those lines crossing his mind when he met Primrose Toplady. It was not that she was monumental in stature: she barely reached five feet. There was nothing of the Amazon in her structure: she was squat and big-busted in an essentially static way. What marked her out was the defiant dignity with which she performed her every movement, even if it was only entering a room with a tray of coffee. She was also an utterly humourless woman – something that she would have denied most vehemently.

Mosley visited her in her upper-working-class-terraced house in that quarter of Bagshawe Broome that is made up entirely of upper-working-class terraces. It was a home of passionate cleanliness and geometrical precision, the principal furniture acquired either just before, during, or immediately after the Second World War. There was a set of Dickens sold at a concessionary price during the newspaper competition of the thirties. There was a home-pegged rug which enlivened the hearth with a prancing tiger. There was a rented colour TV. And there was one concession to casual male comfort: a pair of bedroom slippers on the inside of the brass metal fender. But they lay together with the exact alignment of a soldier's kit laid for barrack inspection. Primrose Toplady had seen five sons and a daughter through to adulthood and there was evidence of this in the range of framed enlargements scattered over walls, shelves and cabinets, showing Topladys of all ages – black and white, hand-tinted and in colour, Topladys building sand-castles, Topladys clasping the parchment of their degree diplomas, Toplady weddings and aerial photographs of Toplady suburban semis.

Mrs Toplady was austerely unpassionate in appearance. It was difficult to picture the sex-life of the Topladys, fruitful though it had been. Kitchener Toplady was a sixteen-stone jowly pachyderm, a wages-clerk at Fothergill's, who towered over his wife – and was distinctly the more disturbed of the two when he saw Mosley on their doorstep.

It was his wife who opened the door, took Mosley's hat and showed Mosley into their tiny front room. Even hovering in the background, Kitchener Toplady looked as if he was in the way. It was to Mrs Toplady that Mosley spoke.

'Henry Burgess –'

Even the initial mention of the name momentarily extracted wind from Mrs Toplady's taut canvas. Her sails did not exactly sag, but their fabric quivered. Mosley did not let it be seen that he had noticed. Her husband, however, was clumsy enough to try to come to her rescue.

'It was too much for her, all that cycling across town in all weathers.'

She behaved as if he had not spoken – or, if he had, as if he was not likely to have made himself understood.

'It was too much for me, all that cycling across town in all weathers,' she said.

Then she launched into a complex account of the financial pressures that had pushed her into the indignity of going out to work: Eric still at university, Katherine at College of Music, Kevin in the sixth form, and her husband *on the sick* and therefore losing overtime.

'The gastric,' Kitchener said.

'The gastric,' she repeated, as if she truly believed that he needed an interpreter.

'How many hours a week did you put in for Henry Burgess?'

'Two every morning, one in the afternoon, but only an hour on Sundays.'

'And I suppose you just did anything that needed doing?'

'Laid and lit his fire. Cooked his breakfast – he always came downstairs on the stroke of nine. Hoovered and tidied him up, did any ironing or mending that was called for.'

'His laundry?'

'I used to bring that home with me.'

'And in the afternoon?'

'Made him a pot of tea. In the darker months I drew his curtains for the evening. Brought him anything he had asked me to get for him from the shops.'

'You never cooked anything for him at midday?'

'He always liked to go out for his lunch.'

Did she sourly disapprove of Henry Burgess's *al fresco* pies? Primrose Toplady was answering every question aseptically, as if she considered it above her station to hold a personal opinion about an employer.

'And for how long did you work for him?'

'Four years, three months and one week.'

'You stopped about two years ago?'

'Two weeks less than two years. It was in November.'

Clearly the break stuck vividly in her memory.

'You left suddenly?'

'I gave notice in the proper fashion.'

'I'm sure you did, Mrs Toplady. What was your immediate reason for leaving?'

'I've told you. All that cycling across town.'

'It must have left a big gap in Henry Burgess's life, not having you arrive according to timetable.'

'I thought very hard about that before I made my mind up.'

'Did he to your knowledge try to get anyone in your place?'

'He wouldn't have found that easy.'

'You think not?'

'Women don't want domestic work these days.'

Mosley knew that that was certainly not true of all local women.

'Perhaps no one wanted to work for Henry Burgess,' he suggested, but she did not rise to that bait.

23

'I've heard him called awkward, nasty-tempered. But you got on all right with him?'

'I never had cause to complain.'

'How much did you see of Henry Burgess after you stopped working for him?'

'I caught sight of him in town from time to time.'

'And you'd pass the time of day?'

'If he saw me. He was often lost in his thoughts.'

'You were still good friends, then?'

Primrose Toplady hesitated. Perhaps it was the word *friend* that threw her. She clearly had her own well-defined code of truthfulness. Mosley knew that it was not by any means the whole truth that she was telling him this morning, but she was the kind of woman who was inhibited from telling the lie direct.

'Mr Burgess was always the most correct of men,' she said.

'I'm sure he was.'

It was difficult to fill in mentally the details of their relationship. Had there been mornings when Burgess had been demonstratively glad to see her? Or had he taken her for granted? Had there been days when he'd barely seemed to notice that she was in his house? What had they ever talked about? Reactionary platitudes triggered off by the morning's headlines? The weather? Or virtually nothing at all?

And had she never been anywhere near Garth since she had left off doing for him? Never gone a hundred yards out of her way on a shopping day to see if he needed anything? Never taken him a little something at Christmas? Never wondered how he was managing, an old man over ninety, who might die in his sleep any night?

Had he perhaps made what amounted to a pass at her – or something that she had construed as a pass? Senile sexuality was a subject in itself, something about which Mosley did not claim to know much, but he knew that it never paid to discount it. Primrose Toplady would have reacted very sharply if anything like that had happened. It was even more difficult to imagine than her and Kitchener in a bout of kittenish love-play.

24

'Did he ever have any visitors to the house while you were working for him?'

'His niece sometimes came and stayed the night – not very often. A very nice lady. Very presentable.'

'And she got on well with her uncle?'

'Very well indeed. She was the only person I knew who could bring him out of himself.'

'How did she manage that?'

'She made jokes. Pretended to lose her patience with him.'

For a moment it looked as if Mrs Toplady was about to loosen up and tell a human anecdote, but she retrieved her self-discipline.

'Of course, she knew how far it was safe to go.'

'Mrs Toplady – when the niece came, did she bring any kind of radio with her – a record-player, or a music centre?'

Mrs Toplady seemed puzzled by the reason for the question. 'I can't say that I remember.'

'Might she have done?'

'I can't say that I'd know the answer to that.'

'What sort of music did Henry Burgess like?'

'Oh, choirs – that sort of thing. Welsh male voices. His favourite was *Myfanwy*.'

'He was very fond of music?'

'Of good music.'

She was still puzzled, was not enjoying this phase of the dialogue. She might know more than she was telling. 'He just enjoyed something good if it came on.'

'And what did he think of this modern stuff?'

'He couldn't stand it. Those groups, those jazzy guitars, young men with long hair – he'd have had the whole lot banned, if he'd had his way.'

'What was his hearing like? Was he going deaf in his old age?'

'Sometimes you'd think so. But he could hear what he wanted to. I had to watch it, I can tell you. If I was doing something in another room – like moving a vase to dust under it, he'd hear. He'd be round the door to make sure I wasn't going to break something.'

Another tiny lifting of the veil, a suggestion that life at

Garth had had its exasperating, even its human moments. But still Mosley did not apply pressure. She was giving him less than a true picture – which amounted to giving him a false picture. But that did not seem to worry him. As he had expounded to Sergeant Beamish, when people wanted to paint a false picture, it paid, if one had the time, to let it develop. It could be useful to know what sort of falseness they wanted to put over.

Mosley transferred his attention to Kitchener.

'It must have been a relief to you to have your wife home again full time.'

This was something of a facer for the dyspeptic Toplady, who was uncertain what his wife would want him to reply.

'I never try to interfere,' he said at last.

Mosley asked one or two more questions, mostly concerned with matters of no apparent relevance, such as Mrs Toplady's route across town on her bicycle and Kitchener's self-medication for his ulcer. Then he seemed to be attaching more importance to the substance of the answers. Had Henry Burgess ever tried to get Primrose Toplady out of his house before the time of her daily stint was up? She shook her head and refused to be dislodged from meeting Mosley's stare.

'There's something that surprises me, Mr and Mrs Toplady.'

They looked at him with round eyes.

'What I can't understand is why neither of you has expressed surprise that I've come here to talk to you this morning.'

Each waited for the other to find something to say.

'Why do you think I have suddenly become interested in the affairs of the late Mr Burgess?'

'I've been wondering about that ever since you rang the door-bell,' Kitchener Toplady said.

'I've been wondering about that myself,' his wife said in innocent support.

'It's something you might like to talk about between yourselves.'

'Well, you know, Mr Mosley – now you mention it –'

'It did sometimes cross my mind at the time –'

26

But Mosley did not seem to be under any press of urgency.

'I think perhaps I've taken you too much by surprise this morning,' he said, with bumbling kindness. 'Perhaps there are things that you'd like to tell me, when you've got them straight in your own minds. Come and see me when you've mulled it all over between yourselves.'

He left the house and made his leisurely way towards Tim Fawcett's office.

Five

Orthodox detection: Mosley established a dusty corner for himself in Bagshawe Broome police station where he asked to see the back numbers of stolen property lists. For half an hour he made notes, then rang HQ at Bradcaster and asked to be put through to Detective-Superintendent Grimshaw.

'I need a sergeant,' he said, addressing his superior by neither rank nor name. There was a rustle of paper in a wire basket, as if that was where Grimshaw kept his reserve manpower.

'Where are you speaking from?'

Mosley paused, as if reluctant to share even as slender a confidence as that.

'Bagshawe Broome.'

'Got something on up there, have you?'

There was a silence at the originating end. Grimshaw wondered if he ought to have known better than to ask.

'Possibly,' Mosley said at last.

'Would you like to expand on that?'

'Can't,' Mosley said. 'Don't know myself yet.'

This time it was Grimshaw who thought before committing himself to speech. A single loose syllable could be fatal.

'Can't let you have Beamish,' he said finally. 'Beamish is up to his neck in it.'

This was received in a silence so long that Grimshaw wondered if Mosley had gone away.

'We think we have a lead,' Grimshaw said, 'on the Soulgate Manor job. Beamish is working on it. I could let

28

you have Dawson for a day or two. Or there's Watson from B Division – a new promotion –'

But this time Mosley really had departed. He made his way across the town to Fawcett and Foster's Office and was observed crossing the Market Place by Miles John Morrison.

Miles Morrison was Bagshawe Broome's most active capitalist, a man whose funds were kept unremittingly at work – and whose portfolio contained nothing in print or writing. Miley was a big man, barrel-chested and with a close-cropped, almost totally bald head. His place of business was a spot five yards south-south-east of Bert Hardcastle's kiosk and ten yards west of the cattle trough, on a corner of which he occasionally sat to receive intelligence or issue his orders of the day. When Miley Morrison was seen sitting with one of his henchmen on a corner of the trough, other men kept their distance, making it plain that they were not trying to eavesdrop. Sometimes Morrison was absent from the Market Place and it was guessed that the return on one of his investments had required personal collection: Morrison knew on which days his clients received their pay-packets, and at precisely what hours they left their places of employment.

There was any amount of speculative legend about Miles Morrison – and there were two incontrovertible known facts, one of which was that he had been to prison. He had served a month for GBH to Wally Schofield, on whose dentures, upper and lower, he had performed such grievous harm that they had had to be written off. Morrison had gone to prison because he had said he would: he had told Wally Schofield to his face and in the hearing of a cuffer that he would do bird for him. It was a long time ago now, and Morrison had never expressed any desire to repeat the experience. But it was a paragraph in his existence that had stood him in good stead ever since. Men liable to offend him, accidentally or otherwise, had not forgotten contemporary accounts of the jags of pink plastic that had emerged through Wally Schofield's cheek. Wally Schofield had owed Miles Morrison ten shillings, and Miles had happened to know that he was in temporary possession of that sum.

The other pertinent fact about Miley Morrison was that he had a family. He had a wife, a tiny, pallid, friendless, screwed-up little woman about whose opinions on any subject nothing was known to a soul. And he had a daughter, Janet, aged thirteen in the year of Henry Burgess's death, who was the neatest-dressed, best scrubbed and most formal-mannered child in Bagshawe Broome. He sent her to a private school in Bradburn and she was seen every morning waiting for her bus in her neat grey uniform and velvet-banded pudding-basin hat.

Whatever surplus was left over from Miles Morrison's weekly profit and loss account was divided with fanatical exactitude into two halves, one of which went into savings for his Janet. The remainder, together with any residue which his wife had managed to squeeze out of their supplementary benefits – which she had to account to him for – was put to immediate work in further speculation. This included an occasional gamble on horses, dogs or forthcoming local events, but was mostly concerned with short-term usury at a monstrous rate of interest. No deal was too petty to be beneath his dignity: he would lend the price of half a pint, or even a sum as low as twenty-five pence, if, say, a man wished to join a syndicate to place an each-way bet. But Morrison had to know that repayment was within the borrower's capacity, and settlement was strictly weekly. Miley opened his books afresh each Friday night, and business was usually languid until about Wednesday.

Miley watched Mosley cross the cobbles towards Fawcett and Foster's, watched him go in at the estate agent's door. Miley was interested – he wanted to know. His prestige – his principal stock in trade – depended on his knowing, or at least appearing to know – everything that happened in Bagshawe. He had even been known to pay small sums to trusted disciples to find things out for him. The impression that he aimed at ideally was that nothing could happen in Bagshawe Broome without his express permission. He knew that Mosley had leaned on Dickie Holgate on Market Day. He knew that Mosley had been asking questions of the landlord of the Lansdowne. He knew that Mosley had been to Bowland Avenue and he knew that he had been to see the

Topladys. And Miley needed to know, before somebody asked him the frontal question – what was going on?

Mosley passed directly in front of Morrison.

'Morning, Mr Mosley.'

Mosley emitted a monosyllabic grunt without turning his head to look at the big man. He had never had anything direct to do with Morrison, had never given the impression that he took cognizance of Morrison's existence. He opened the door of Fawcett's office, closely watched by Morrison.

In contrast to his behaviour on Market Day, Desmond Lummis, Tim Fawcett's young man, almost fawned over Mosley. Mr Fawcett was away for the day, valuing stock for the take-over of an inn up one of the Lake District passes, but if there was anything he could do –

'Aye, well, it's this tackle that old Henry Burgess left –'

'Oh, yes, Mr Mosley –'

'I take it that not all the small stuff was made over for Dickie Holgate to dispose of –'

'Oh, no – not by any means. We always make it a point to let him have a few things he can expect to make something on – but there were one or two items worth putting into one of our own sales.'

'Such as?'

There was an influx of sharpness in Mosley's tone that made the young man look keenly at him.

'Let's have a look at your list, shall we?'

Lummis went to a cabinet and brought out a file, which he seemed to think that he and Mosley were going to read together. But Mosley took it over to the window, as if it needed daylight. When he came back with it he brought out a notebook and made a laborious business of noting down three items.

'Where are these articles now?'

A nineteenth-century silver tankard in mock-Elizabethan style; a colour-printed plate by Pratt of Fenton; a ceremonial sword, HM Diplomatic Service –

'They are in our strong-vault, over in our auction rooms.'

'I fear I shall have to relieve you of them for the time being. Against receipt of course. And Mrs Nancy Batham – Henry Burgess's niece? I take it there'd be one or two small objects she took a fancy to, and that didn't go forward to the sale or to Dickie Holgate?'

'I'd have no paper record of anything like that,' Lummis said.

'No – of course you wouldn't,' Mosley said, not without a touch of malice. 'Those things would have changed hands before the District Valuer put his nose in, wouldn't they?'

Lummis looked uneasy.

Don't worry. We live and let live – sometimes,' Mosley said.

He next reappeared in the Market Place carrying the objects, roughly parcelled, under his arm. Miley Morrison had transferred himself to his throne on the cattle trough, where he was in solemn consultation with a small man in a cloth cap whose features had the foxiness of a happy mental defective. Miley missed nothing of Mosley's movements. He watched the inspector go over to speak to Harry Bamber, who was about to get aboard his milk-float. They were too far away for Miley to hear what was being said.

'Can you remember, Harry, what sort of an order you used to deliver to Henry Burgess?'

'Pint a day ever since I've been on the job. All except when Mrs Toplady was doing for him. Then it was a pint and a half, bar Sundays. And six eggs every Monday morning.'

'Never any more than that?'

'Funny you should mention that, Mr Mosley.'

'You don't seem to be laughing?'

'You know what I mean, Mr Mosley. Twice – no, three times – he put out more empties than usual – oh, say half a dozen. And I thought to myself, the old bugger must have thrown a party. Only they weren't my bottles. Foreigners. Gledholt Dairies, over in Yorkshire. Ripon. That's it – Ripon.'

'When was this?'

'Oh, now you've got me. Fair while ago now.'

'Before or after Mrs Toplady's day?'

'During her time. I expect she was the one who put them out – having a clear-out. They could have been in the house a long time. But it struck me as odd – all that milk from as far off as Ripon.'

32

'I expect there's a perfectly feasible explanation.'

'I expect there is, Mr Mosley.'

Mosley next loitered in the vicinity of the municipal refuse collectors, waiting to pounce on a round-shouldered little Pakistani who was carrying rubbish out of a chemist's shop in an old zinc bath.

'Nah, Neddy.'

'Nah, Mr Mosley.'

The Asiatic spoke with true local vowels, but with his countrymen's timbre of extreme politeness.

'Dickinson Road, Neddy. Bowland Avenue. Were you ever on that round?'

'Every Thursday, Mr Mosley.'

'Ever pick up anything unusual in Bowland Avenue?'

'Unusual, Mr Mosley?'

'I was thinking of the old man who lived alone in the big house. Did he ever throw anything away that you wouldn't expect an old man to have?'

The Pakistani laughed.

'We found a pair of pink knickers once. And the week after that it was nylon tights. It was a funny word the foreman used. What was it, now? Transvestite, that's it. He said old Henry must be turning into a transvestite.'

Mosley walked a few yards along the pavement and stood for some moments looking intently but remotely over at Veronique's Boutique. Veronique's Boutique had a ribald reputation in Bagshawe Broome. It was remarkable how overstaffed the shop seemed to be with bedworthy young saleswomen, and how many men went in whom one would be surprised to know to have legitimate purchases to make there. Then he turned away as if he had either learned nothing or made no decision, moved off with unhurried dignity towards the police station, still carrying the tankard, the plate and the ceremonial sword.

He rang a police station in one of the smaller towns and asked if Detective-Sergeant Beamish was on the premises. He was not. He was out on duty.

'Ask him to phone me here at Bagshawe Broome as soon as he comes in. I'll wait here till he does.'

As soon as Mosley had left the Market Place, Miles

Morrison unseated himself from the trough and ambled like a *High Noon* duellist towards the dust-cart. When Miley moved anywhere except between the trough and his spot south-south-east of Bert Hardcastle's kiosk, it was a signal of impending events. Men looked on with focused interest. Miley put a hand like a bear's paw on the shoulder of the Pakistani.

'What did he want?'

'Who, Mr Morrison?'

'Mosley.'

'He was asking about Bowland Avenue.'

'What's up in Bowland Avenue?'

'Nothing's up there, Mr Morrison. He was asking if we ever found anything there.'

'And what did you tell him?'

'A pair of pink knickers, sir, and some nylon tights.'

'Are you trying to take the piss out of me?'

Morrison moved his free hand suddenly. The Pakistani cowered.

'No, Mr Morrison, sir. You know me, Mr Morrison.'

Miley went back to the mental defective on the trough.

Mosley sat writing copious notes in the police station. It was two hours before Beamish rang.

'I have it on unimpeachable authority, Sergeant Beamish, that you have a vested interest in the Soulgate Manor job.'

'Don't tell me you've –'

'I've got a few of the bits and pieces here.'

'I'm on my way.'

Mosley went over to Bert Hardcastle's for a sandwich.

Six

It would be the ruin of Beamish, Detective-Superintendent Grimshaw had said.

It was a matter of indifference to Mosley and Beamish whether they were going to prove the making or unmaking of each other. After several spells of case-work together, they had become friends, each learning to anticipate the other's mind – and each deriving an occasional flush of pleasure at the success of his as opposed to the other's system.

Mosley showed Beamish his collection of fenced *objets d'art*, and Beamish saw at once that it was no mere matter of retrieval that was satisfying the inspector.

'This is the first connection we've picked up between the two cases,' he said.

'Let's not leap before we've looked. It could possibly be two sets of villains getting rid of their stuff through the same receiver. Yet I can't help thinking –'

'It's the same sort of loot. What about the *modus operandi*?'

'It wasn't so much a *modus operandi* as sheer opportunism: move in and take what's there.'

'I know next to nothing about the Lytham St Anne's break-in. Lytham's not our territory.'

'They sent us carbon copies, just in case. It was one of those well-to-do houses on the front. Near the windmill. Do you know Lytham? Owners away for the winter. In the Canaries. The evidence isn't clear about how many people

35

took part. It was either four who spent a fortnight in the house, or two for a month. Or *pro rata*.'

'They lived in the place?'

'Squatted. Very skilfully – yet of course without respect for the house or anything in it. None of the neighbours had an inkling that there was anyone on the premises – yet they left behind a minor mountain of filth: convenience food packets, stinking food cans, empty wine-bottles – lying about under beds, stuffed in wardrobes. Aerosolled graffiti on brocaded wall-paper and moulded ceilings. Of course, it may not have been too difficult lying doggo. Those houses have well-enclosed gardens.'

'Like Dickinson Road and Bowland Avenue?'

'Precisely.'

'So you think there's been someone living in Bowland Avenue since Henry Burgess's death?'

'On the contrary. I think they struck camp when the old man died. But God knows how long he'd had house-guests.'

Beamish whistled between his teeth. There was still a sparkle of boyishness about him. When he was impressed, he was apt to react openly.

'They didn't squat in Soulgate Manor. They were in and out within an hour. We know that from local statements. They did the job while the owners were dining out – and they got in by battering-ram tactics – no subtlety at all.'

'How many of them?'

'No reliable evidence. I wouldn't have said more than two, actually inside the house. You could perhaps add a driver and a look-out.'

'And only small things taken?'

'Strictly portables only.'

'And the loot eventually trickles into Garth, Bowland Avenue, Bagshawe Broome. Some of it's exposed for sale on Bagshawe Market. I have a gut feeling. Let's go and look over what's left in Garth. You might recognize something you've heard described.'

They walked along Dickinson Road, poorly lit and deserted at nine-o'clock in the evening, not even a retired citizen walking his dog. The inhabitants of the big houses – many of which had now been adapted as blocks of flats –

were all securely armchaired in front of *Dallas* or Hurricane Higgins – except, that is, for one man.

It was the movement of this man's foot against fallen leaves that gave him away. He had been doing his best to merge into the foliage in a deep-set gateway, but immediately he knew that he had been seen, he optimistically changed his tactics and stepped out into full view as Mosley and Beamish were almost upon him.

'Good evening, Mr Mosley. Evening, Mr Er –'

It was Miles Morrison – hundreds of significant yards removed from his normal orbit of activity.

'A trifle off-course, aren't we, Miley?' Mosley asked him aggressively. But Miley opted for the soft, bright answer.

'I do quite a bit of walking on fine evenings these days, Mr Mosley. There's no need for anything as violent as jogging. I always say that a brisk walk –'

'You weren't walking just now, Miley. You were skulking.'

'Oh, come now, Mr Mosley. Skulking's not a nice word. I stop every twenty minutes to do deep breathing exercises. I was reading in one of my wife's magazines –'

'Keep it up, Miley. You'll need to be in the best of health when I finally catch up with you.'

They walked smartly on. Behind them they heard Morrison set out back towards the town centre in the direction from which they had come, hoping no doubt to convince them that he had not been about to show an interest in Bowland Avenue.

'We won't go straight there,' Mosley said. 'I'd like to go in by the back way for more than one reason.'

So he took Beamish by a public footpath between houses to Westwood Park, where he had confounded two old-age pensioners by disappearing through the privet two days ago. But he did not pay any attention at first to the back end of Henry Burgess's garden. Instead, he led them towards a side-road that petered out drearily along the western boundary of the park. It was a dismal end of nowhere because, like Bowland Avenue, the road-making had never been finished. But there was a difference. Bowland Avenue had never been made-up because old Bowland had never intended that it should be. But this other road – Westlands Way – was a projected extension of an estate that had been abandoned in mid-construction, sub-contractors unpaid, in the recession of the 1970s. The last house to be finished was seventy-five yards away, and the road from there to here had been left half concreted. Some of its kerbstones had been laid – or partially laid. The footings of some of the houses, and markers for their gardens, had long been overgrown. Concrete had cracked and crumbled in hard winters. Trenches dug for drains had been left unfilled-in, leaving weather and weeds to do the job unevenly.

'We've work to do here by daylight,' Mosley said. 'Or at least you have. Asking around at those houses up there. I've been wondering how they managed their transport problem. They must have had wheels of some sort or other and they must have had somewhere inconspicuous to park. I've already found how they got into old Henry's garden. I disappeared through that rabbit-hole on Saturday afternoon, quickly enough to risk giving two old 'uns a heart-attack apiece.'

He had not gone through a gap in the privet. There was a trenched groove, scooped out under the hedge between two of its more widely-spaced roots. It could afford very rapid entry for an athletic man – and even the less than agile Mosley made short work of it.

The garden was damp, with clammy spiders' webs that fell across their faces. A feral cat fled over an avalanche of loose rubbish into deep shadow. Beamish touched Mosley's sleeve.

'There's someone in the house.'

There was the faint movement of a source of light in one of the upstairs rooms. While they were watching, the torch disappeared from the bedroom, and evidently the door was closed behind it.

'It might be Dickie Holgate,' Mosley said. 'He's got a fair amount of property to collect from here and he's not likely to do that during valuable trading hours.'

But after five minutes in which there was no further manifestation, he changed his mind.

'If it was young Holgate, he'd have shown himself again

by now. He wouldn't be taking pains to conceal himself. I'll stay here. You go round to the front. If you do see anyone, play it by ear. If all's quiet, come back here in an hour.'

Left alone, Mosley sat down on a pile of rubble, patient and motionless. An owl hooted in one of the trees in the Park. The cat, taking courage, stalked back to its original ambush. A shoot of overgrown rambler tapped arhythmically against a window pane. There was no further sign of movement in the house. Mosley's breathing was slow, deep and regular. Then somewhere in the night a woman screamed. It was in front of the house, but it was not loud and it was not prolonged. Mosley did not stir. He was happy to leave this to Beamish.

The sergeant was back very shortly after that, characteristically elated and carrying something in a white plastic bag that reflected what light there was in the night.

'I'm afraid I've given an old lady rather a scare. I was standing back in the shadows, and she came out of the front door of Garth – quite openly – and out of the garden gate as if she had every right to be using it.'

'There's no other way in which she could come out. What sort of old lady?'

'Well, when I say *old*, she could have been anything from her mid-fifties to mid-sixties. Rather a pompous and self-conscious little soul, I'd say.'

'*Stately as a galleon*?'

'I beg your pardon?'

'Don't you know that song? Round glasses, shelving bosom, moves like royalty on walkabout?'

'You've got her.'

'Primrose Toplady.'

'I'm afraid she thought she was about to be mugged. And for good measure I sort of flapped my raincoat at her. She started to scream – I've no doubt you heard her – so I clapped my hand over her mouth – not roughly. The moment I released her, she shot along Dickinson Road. She dropped this.'

He held out the plastic.

'So I suppose we shall have a patrol out here in no time.' he said apologetically.

'I doubt it. Mrs Toplady won't be drawing attention to whatever she's been up to. I'm glad you didn't give chase. It would have been premature to have caught her.'

'Well, she seemed so obviously local, I felt sure we'd have no difficulty tracing her. And it would surely be better to do that in daylight – after passions have cooled.'

'What was it she dropped?'

'I looked at them under a street lamp. It's a pair of china dogs, one of them smashed beyond repair. I wouldn't think they have much value. They're not even nice china dogs. They don't even look doggy. Whoever designed them just didn't appreciate a dog.'

'You shall have the supreme pleasure of returning them to her in the morning,' Mosley said, 'and asking her any embarrassing questions that come into your head. I think you'll quite enjoy a session with Primrose Toplady. Let's attend to Garth now, shall we?'

Mosley had a small but quite useful collection of picklocks in his pocket, but the back door was bolted on the inside. The window catches were amateurishly but firmly wired up.

'I got in by the front door on Saturday. The latch was no trouble. But it's a pity to keep advertising our presence. I dare say Miley is still keeping look-out.'

'Uh huh!' Beamish said suddenly.

Someone else had entered the house – this time without precautions. Mosley thumped at the kitchen window, rattling it violently in its frame.

'Let us in, Dickie!'

Dickie Holgate drew the bolts and stood grinning at them.

'What would you have done if I hadn't shown up?'

But Mosley seemed disinclined to fraternize with him.

'Never mind about that. You just get on with whatever work you've come here to do.'

'All right, Inspector. Be like that.'

Then he caught sight of the fragments of china dog that Beamish had just brought out of the bag to examine more closely.

'Here – what are you doing with those? They belong on the kitchen mantelpiece. I could have got a good price for them.'

'One of them's still in mint condition,' Beamish told him.

'It needs to be a pair.'

'I've a feeling they weren't yours to sell in any case,' Mosley said. 'But I'll accept your plea of innocence in this particular instance.'

'Mr Mosley –'

It seemed to Beamish that Mosley was going out of his way to rib Holgate, and Holgate was playing into his hands by letting his irritation show. The young dealer stamped into another room and came back carrying various objects which he set down noisily on a table under Mosley's nose. They included two small mantel decorations in butterfly-wing, a set of pewter spirit-measures and a silver-plated musical box surmounted by a now wounded Dresden ballerina.

'You were on at me about not studying your loot lists properly, Inspector. It's a pity you don't read them yourself before you send them out. I've been doing a bit of belated homework, and I think you'll find that these have all figured in the last twelve months.'

Mosley glanced at the objects as if they did not greatly interest him.

'Beginning to develop a conscience, are you, Master Holgate? Or getting cold feet?'

'It seems to me,' Beamish said to Mosley afterwards, 'that you stuck a lot of pins into that young man's bottom just for the hell of it. He stands high on the suspect list, does he?'

'He doesn't appear on it at all. As honest as you could expect a man in his walk of life to be.'

'What, then?'

Mosley stopped to scrape dottle from his pipe into the gutter. They were walking back along Dickinson Road.

'You think I've got my fingers on the pulse of this town, don't you, Sergeant Beamish?'

'Well, I'd say that if anybody has – '

'There are men who will talk to me. Some of them may even talk to you, once they're accustomed to your face. They will tell us many things, perhaps even some things that they believe to be true. But what they tell us will be restricted to what they care for us to know. You and I are due to get a great deal of help in the next few days – but some of it is likely to be misleading help. Because the key men in Bagshawe Broome do not themselves know what has been going on. That is beginning to worry them. They will need to satisfy their own curiosity before they can decide how much it is safe to pass on to us. Therefore I want young Mr Holgate to think he is in imminent danger of a miscarriage of justice. He will quickly come to the conclusion that he has only one really reliable defence, and that is to find out for himself who has been trafficking in this stuff. You do see, don't you, sergeant, that he is in a much stronger position to do that than we are?'

Mosley hiccoughed. He was still having trouble getting a draught through his pipe. He stopped to do further, fundamental excavation.

'And Holgate isn't the only one who'll be trying to get down to taproots. Another will be the character we met while we were on our way to Bowland Avenue.'

'The big chap?'

'There's no need to be scared of Miley Morrison. He'd crumble like a house of cards if you waved a paper fan at him.'

'I'm sure he would.'

'Good! I'm glad you think that. Because you might have to wave something more than a fan at him before we've finished.'

42

Seven

By the morning, Beamish had thought his way into a minor
anxiety state about a number of things. It was all very well
Mosley treating him as if his transfer to Bagshawe Broome
were already a *fait accompli*. He knew very well from
experience how facts came to be accomplished by Mosley's
Law. They could not always be managed with similar
equanimity by an ambitious young officer who did not wish
to compromise himself irreversibly with the top office.
Beamish walked into Bagshawe Broome police station
intending to talk firmly – though of course in the friendliest
fashion – to Mosley. It was true that a few minor items from
Soulgate had turned up here, but they were only peripheral
to other aspects that Beamish had in hand. There was, for
example, the plaster-cast of a sole-print that he was still
trying to narrow down through manufacturers and retailers.
There was a sheaf of local statements that might still be
made to deliver something under computer analysis: if he
could only think of the right questions to programme in.
There were various sightings of an ancient brown Ford
Classic saloon. And all this seemed more likely to bear fruit
than did a pompous little woman carrying two china dogs in
a plastic bag whom he had scared into thinking that he was a
streaking mugger. And that was saying nothing about the
sort of future that lay in needling a six-foot, barrel-chested
hoodlum surrounded by his sycophants in a one-horse
market place. So Mosley had to be reasoned with. If Mr
Grimshaw thought that he could be usefully employed for a

day or two in Bagshawe Broome, then that was all right by Beamish. Otherwise –

But Mosley remained in command of the situation by one of his favourite devices, which Beamish had known him put to devastating use in the past. He was not in Bagshawe Broome police station at the hour when he had told Beamish to meet him there. Bagshawe police station did not know where Mosley was. Beamish hung about for half an hour, desperately unhappy to be idle.

So Beamish decided to get on with the first chore that Mosley had given him: to ask around in the few houses on the unfinished estate west of Westwood Park. Could anyone remember anything about a suspiciously parked car? An unspecified period of months ago?

Beamish walked out to the estate. The central avenue and its partial herringbone of closes (all named, without any thought of geographical juxtaposition, after United Kingdom mountains) looked if anything more dispirited even than the area left derelict by the bankrupt builder. Even inhabited walls seemed to exist in an envelope of suspended animation. There were people about: mothers returning from taking their children to school, wheeling their younger infants back home in tin-wheeled buggies. A window in someone's upstairs room had been broken and repaired with a side of potato-crisp carton. The beginnings of disrepair had encouraged a spreading negligence. One or two gardens had been pathetically planted with shrubs now leggy and undernourished. In others a start at cultivation had been abandoned. In some no effort had been made to clear away the initial dressing of contractors' rubble. Here was a child's swing. There a clutch of moulting pigeons was perched on blistered roofing felt. An eclectic gang of dejected dogs chased each other from garden to garden, reverting already to pack-law.

Beamish approached a knot of women who seemed unable to part from each other on the corner of Skiddaw and Carnedd Dafydd. He introduced himself and saw that one was dark-skinned but of European feature and had one black and one creamy-white baby. A white woman, on the other hand, was pushing two piccaninnies who might have stepped from the pages of Harriet Beecher Stowe. The others were local lasses who had been at the neighbourhood comprehensive not so many years – or months – ago. The ethnic assortment did not affect Beamish, but the women might have been talking in code, for all he was able to make out about the subject of their debate.

'I'm here making enquiries about a car.'

They looked at him without interest, without curiosity. One of them was already making ready to move away, jockeying to straighten her wheels on the up-rising slabs of the pavement.

'Have any of you ever noticed a car that doesn't seem to belong to anyone on the estate?'

They were not only silent – there seemed something mournful about their silence. He nodded his head in the direction of the park railings.

'Maybe it was parked down there, a long way from any of your houses.'

None of them seemed to care whether such a vehicle had ever existed.

'What I'm talking about may have been some time ago.'

There was not even a look of consultation between one pair of eyes and another. He was aware of the ineptitude of his questions. The women failed to show even a willingness to think about them.

'Do you often see strangers on or about this estate?'

One woman, surprisingly, did reply to that. She had an unusually high-pitched voice, in which the local vowels and glottal stops sounded oddly out of place.

'A new tallyman came collecting dues last week for the *Golden Treasury* catalogue. He doesn't look as if he'll last even as long as the last one did. It's a firm that likes results.'

Laughter: they were not entirely devoid of wit.

'There was a mini parked all night one night last week outside Felicity Wood's. Her old man's in hospital with gallstones.'

You're only jealous because it wasn't parked outside yours, Kathy.'

More laughter. If only he could keep them in as happy a frame of mind as this –

'I wasn't thinking,' Beamish said, 'of anyone actually coming to your doors. Somebody who'd drive down there past the last house, then perhaps go off through the Park.'

No one had anything to volunteer.

'No?'

He gave them another chance for some memory to vibrate. Nothing emerged. Nothing was going to emerge.

'Well, thank you, ladies.'

They laughed a third time, unified again by the sight of his ineffectiveness as he turned his back on them and walked down through the wilderness of the unbuilt zone. He came to the opposite side of the fence where he and Mosley had stood looking outwards yesterday. And there he did see something. It was a patch of bare earth between two scraggy clumps of ragwort. Some vehicle had stood there, leaking from sump or crankshaft. Beamish thought it might be an idea to take a small sample of the oil-soaked soil. There were circumstances in which he could see it coming in useful. He had an optimistic faith in forensic science. It had never brought him a miracle result yet, but he lived in hope. He was stooping to fill one of his little plastic envelopes when a voice from behind him startled him.

'What's this, then? Sherlock Holmes himself?'

A bald-headed man in a shabby brown pullover: Beamish did not know him at the time, but he was to hear plenty about him later in the day at the police station.

E. Jones, thirty years timekeeper at Caudwells', made redundant when they went on short time. E. Jones, who had not done a paid hour's work (that they knew about at the *Labour*) since he was in his late forties. E. Jones, busybody, prodnose and malcontent. E. Jones, whose volume of correspondence in the local press ought to have come to the notice of Norris McWhirter. Scarcely a week passed but that the *Bagshawe Guardian* published a letter signed by their obedient servant, E. Jones. *I feel it is my duty to inform you* was his favourite opening formula, and E. Jones's sense of duty had in its time been called to action stations by pavement-fouling Labradors, unlighted street-lamps, over-illuminated electricity showrooms and the moral decadence he had observed behind a shrubbery in Westwood Park through his cross-channel binoculars.

'You're not from round these parts,' E. Jones informed Beamish, fishing for information.

'County CID.'

'You're about five months too late, that's all.'

E. Jones's sense of duty was already composing a paragraph about police procrastination.

'That was when a car last stood there?'

'Five months – give or take half an hour or so.'

'Can you tell me anything about the owners?'

'Never saw them. Must always have come by night.'

'They came often, then? Regularly?'

'Three or four times altogether, perhaps a month or two apart. Must have stayed a week or so each time. I can't give you all the dates, but you can get an idea if you go and consult the *Guardian* files. I wrote them a letter, complaining. I felt it my duty to draw the attention of the authorities to car-dumping. That's what I thought it was, car-dumping. If you'd asked me, I'd never have said the damned crate would start again. It certainly hadn't many more miles in it.'

'I hope you took its registration numbers?'

'It had none. No plates, even. No licence disc. Not even a door-handle on the front passenger side: tied up with string. Odometer said 90,000 odd miles – but who knows how many times the bugger had been round?'

'Did you not report it to the police?'

'Aye. They came and looked, said something about having it towed away. Next morning it was gone, and I thought that's what they'd done. Till it showed up afresh.'

'Did you report it a second time?'

'What was the bloody point? It didn't seem they'd taken any notice the first bloody time.'

'You can tell me what make it was?'

'Ford Classic. Brown. Shit brown. Like this pullover.'

Beamish began to think that there might be some point in hanging round Mosley until further notice.

Mosley was at the police station when Beamish returned there, laughing his head off with the desk sergeant.

'Ah,' Mosley said, incorporating into the single sound an unanswerable refutation of everything that Beamish might have had it in mind to say.

'Ah,' Beamish agreed, conscious that he had conveyed no meaning in the syllable.

'This is what I like to see – a sergeant up and on his rounds betimes.'

'And well worth while, as it happens.'

With typical rising eagerness, Beamish told what he had unearthed on the Mountains Estate. Mosley, unexpectedly, set in at once to douse his enthusiasm.

'You're talking as if you'd closed the case-file, sergeant.'

'No – but I regard this as an achievement – dare I say, a breakthrough?'

'If you consider this a breakthrough, I'd hate to see you when you're stuck. All you've done is confirm what we already know: that Garth was used as a transit camp and store by some unknown person.'

'Nevertheless –'

'What you are really trying to say is that you have discovered for yourself – or rediscovered – what I as good as told you yesterday.'

'But I've come across reports of this brown Ford Classic before – seen by witnesses near the Soulgate Manor on the night in question.'

'It would be a little surprising if it hadn't been seen by somebody, wouldn't it? All you've got to do now is to circulate the details and wait for some patrol to pull it in.'

'Yes, well, I know, of course, that we need more –'

'We need much more,' Mosley said. 'And your next call has to be on Primrose Toplady.'

It was unusual for Mosley to treat him as pugnaciously as this. Beamish was tempted to think that he was trying to show off in front of the Bagshawe station staff.

'I'm on my way to the Topladys in the next five minutes. But there is one thing, Inspector Mosley. Don't you think that this ought to be cleared with Mr Grimshaw?'

'What do you want to go clearing things with Tom Grimshaw for?'

'I *am* answerable to him.'

'Do you want to be whisked away from Bagshawe Broome before the morning's out, Sergeant Beamish?'

'Naturally not.'

'Then leave me to do the worrying about Grimshaw. Now about the Topladys: a very worried couple, Sergeant. So you have everything made for you. Five or six times already they've tried to get in touch with me this morning. That's why you may have had a little difficulty in contacting me. I prefer not to be available to the Topladys for some little time.'

'Why is that, Inspector?'

'Because their relief when they finally do get hold of me will be so great that they'll be ready to tell me anything. Especially after they've had the traumatic experience of a visit from you.'

'I don't see there's any call to put it quite like that.'

'That's how it had better be, though, if you want to get anywhere.'

Before the ladies of the Mountain Estate had set out for school with their children, one figure familiar in the Bagshawe landscape was already setting out on her daily journey.

Janet Morrison, scrubbed, her hair drawn tightly into pigtails, immaculate in her neat grey uniform and velvet-banded pudding-basin hat, was waiting on the pavement for the Bradburn bus.

It was a trying journey on the icy-draughted, frosty, foggy mornings that were prominent in the Bagshawe climate, and Janet always looked chilled and peaky, a perpetually unhappy child. She never spoke to anyone. Sometimes people wondered whether she even spoke at home or school. Some thought she was toffee-nosed, but this was a phrase that they never allowed to rise to their lips, her father being who and what he was. No one knew precisely what future Miley thought he had lined up for his daughter, but it was evident that he did not permit any aberration from the narrow uphill path that he saw as leading to it. She seemed to have no friends: no other child from Bagshawe went to St

Christopher's private school in Bradburn. It was not clear what researches had led Miley to prefer its educational advantages. Perhaps it was because it was several walls removed from Bagshawe Broome.

There was seldom an unfamiliar face on the early bus from Bagshawe to Bradburn: it was not a service used by anyone who was not compelled to. But there was an occasional exception, and today was one of those days. There were two strangers, sitting on the opposite side of the upper deck from Janet Morrison, and obliquely behind her, so that if they had wished to position themselves to keep her under observation, they could scarcely have done better.

They were young people, perhaps in their early twenties. The man had a giant and brilliant green cockade of hair, and a pair of nail-scissors hanging as a modest ornament from the lobe of his left ear. The girl's hair totally obscured her face and she was wearing a very long and very dirty sleeveless patchwork coat whose hem flopped over her hobnailed boots.

Such phenomena were not entirely uncommon in Bagshawe Broome nowadays, but they still caused passengers on the buses to draw a little more tightly into their own seats.

Eight

At the sight of Sergeant Beamish on her doorstep Primrose Toplady threw her fingers to her mouth as if she were slapping back a scream. Undoubtedly, Beamish reflected, she had something to scream about. At first sight, she was being visited in her home by a man who yesterday evening had given every appearance of being about to ravish her on the corner of Dickinson Road and Bowland Avenue.

She tried to slam her door, but a smart movement of one foot over the threshold is one of the first lessons in the training of all social workers, health visitors, door-to-door canvassers – and policemen. In the same moment, Beamish brought out his warrant card, which he had ready, palmed away in his raincoat pocket. She peered down at it, but he did not think that it was registering.

'I think you'd better read it carefully, Mrs Toplady. I am Sergeant Beamish, CID, at present working from Bagshawe Broome police station.'

Did even this register? As a more concrete suggestion, he held up the white plastic bag.

'Don't you think you'd better ask me in, Mrs Toplady?'

She was still uncertain, but even in her distrust, she lost nothing of her dignity. There was something of the capital ship cleared for action even in a Primrose Toplady who more than half believed that she was on the brink of sexual outrage. But she was not thinking fast this morning.

'Sergeant –'

She had forgotten his name already – if she had taken it in.

51

'Beamish.'

'Sergeant Beamish. I wish to speak to one of your superiors. I wish to speak to Inspector Mosley.'

'About last night?'

'Of course it is about last night.'

'What time last night?'

'You know very well what time it was.'

'Where, last night?'

'You know very well where. On the corner of Dickinson Road and –'

'You do not deny, then, that you were in that part of town last night?'

'You know very well where I was.'

'Coming out of the grounds of a house in Bowland Avenue. My reason for being here, Mrs Toplady, is to ask you what right you had to be in that house and to bring property out of it.'

She began to moisten her lower lip, and then apparently thought better of doing anything that might suggest she had the fidgets.

'I need to know whether you had lawful cause to be where you were, doing what you were doing. So might we try to clear that up? We can do it here on the doorstep if you like. Or we could go to the police station, where you might even get a chance to speak to Inspector Mosley; though I did hear him tell someone that he would be out most of the day.'

He won. He knew that she wanted him out of sight of the neighbours at all costs. Leading him like a diminutive drum-major, she showed him to a chair in the sitting-room, which was also a portrait-gallery of young Topladys at all stages of their development.

'Now, Mrs Toplady. Yesterday evening I saw you coming out of the house called Garth.'

'I used to work there, Sergeant Beamish.'

'And you still have authority to enter the house?'

She made no answer.

'Have you, Mrs Toplady? Have you authority to enter it?'

'The house *is* empty, Sergeant.'

'The house is far from empty. Last night it contained, among other things, a pair of white china dogs.'

52

This time she could not restrain her lip-moistening.

'I can explain what I was doing with the dogs, Mr Beamish.'

'Do that, then, please.'

'They are *my* dogs, Mr Beamish. They belong to me.'

'Indeed? And how do a pair of china dogs belonging to you come to be in Mr Burgess's house?'

Had she perhaps taken them there at the apogee of her housekeepership to enhance the quality of Henry Burgess's life? What, Beamish wondered, had he thought of them?

'I suppose I've been rather silly, Mr Beamish. I don't know whether you'll ever believe me.'

'You have two chances, Mrs Toplady.'

'Mr Burgess used to have two china dogs on his kitchen mantelpiece. They were Staffordshire ware, and had belonged to his wife. He was always telling me how valuable they were.'

'Not *these* dogs?'

'No. I am coming to that. One day I broke one of them – one of Mr Burgess's – while I was dusting. I simply daren't tell him, Mr Beamish: he could be very hasty-tempered. So I went out and bought two more. They weren't really much like the original ones, but Mr Burgess's eyesight was not all it might be. He never went to the kitchen mantelpiece for anything. I hoped that at a distance he might not notice that anything had changed. And – well – I was lucky – he didn't.'

'So you thought you'd go in and get them back?'

'Well, they *are* mine. I did pay for them.'

'And had you repaid Mr Burgess for the breakage?'

Mrs Toplady did not like the question.

'Tell me how you got into the house, Mrs Toplady.'

She liked that one even less.

'Come along, Mrs Toplady.'

'I still had a key.'

'From when you used to work for Mr Burgess? Did he know that you had kept it?'

'I don't suppose he ever thought about it.'

'Mrs Toplady – I'm sure I don't have to point out to you –'

Her embarrassment was cumulative. She was blushing now.

'Mr Beamish – the day I left, I forgot to give it back. I was so flustered. When I did remember, I kept promising myself I'd go round with it. But I kept putting it off.'

Beamish was not satisfied. There was something wrong somewhere. How does a policeman know that a subject is not telling him the truth? It is a print-out from that complex albeit technologically imperfect data-bank that is a policeman's brain. An unwillingness to look one in the eye; or, in the case of some personalities, an unnatural determination to look one in the eye. A self-conscious tone of voice. A constant fretful touching of chin, nose or knee. Perspiration. Uncalled-for emphasis. Primrose Toplady was not sending any of the standard signals – but she was not at ease.

'So what's going to happen now?' she asked, her confidence now visibly on the ebb.

'That I can't tell you. I shall make my report to Inspector Mosley, but the ultimate decision will be made by the superintendent.'

'I haven't committed any crime.'

'Technically you have, in my belief. But I can't see anyone taking a very serious view of it.'

Mosley had wanted Mrs Toplady to be disturbed and contrasts could help by confusing her. Beamish decided to give her a short respite.

'We shall have to get this all down on paper presently: but I would not let it worry you. I can't help thinking that retrieving you own property won't be treated as the crime of the century.'

'Oh, I couldn't stand the shame of having to go to court. I shan't have to go to court, shall I?'

'Not necessarily. The superintendent has broad discretion in cases like this. He could let you off with a caution.'

Beamish began to take a benign interest in the pictures with which the room was over-embellished.

'A large family you have, Mrs Toplady.'

'Well, yes – we've enjoyed watching them grow up. And every one a credit to us, though I say it myself. But what are *they* going to think? Will it get into the newspapers?'

Beamish got up and picked up a frame that was standing on the television set.

'Which one is this?'

'That's Eric. The eldest. He teaches French in Lincolnshire. He has two children – one doing his A levels this year. Doesn't time fly?'

'It certainly does. And this one?'

'That's Charles. He's the sporting one of the family. He had trials for Preston while he was still at school, but his father managed to persuade him that football is better as a hobby than as master. The young lady with the 'cello is Grace, our only girl. She's librarian with a symphony orchestra. Then there's Bruce. He does research in leather dyes. He has a chemistry degree from Leeds university.'

'There's one here standing on his head.'

'That's Brian. We always call him the family stand-up comic. There's never a dull moment when Brian's around. Mr Beamish – could we come back to what we were talking about just now?'

'By all means, Mrs Toplady.'

'I think I may have been a little stupid, but I've never robbed anybody.'

'I really wouldn't worry too much. Just wait and see what happens. Perhaps nothing will. How many children had you altogether?'

'Six. Including, as I told you, just the one girl.'

Beamish looked round the walls and ledges again with some puzzlement.

'Funny. I may be making some mistake, but if you asked me, I'd say I can only count five.'

She stood up, came and looked round herself, as if it puzzled her that there should be a puzzle.

'Ah, yes – I see what you mean. It's Kevin. He always disappears when he sees anybody with a camera, does Kevin. He's done that all his life. He's our youngest – and I'm afraid everybody spoiled him – especially his sister. Look – he's in this one.'

Kevin was barely discernible in a group in an enlargement of a badly conceived snapshot: a boy of about ten, screwing up his eyes against direct sunlight.

'What's Kevin doing now?'

'He's the unlucky one. He wasn't allowed to finish his degree. His college cut down on numbers at the end of his first year. I don't think that was at all fair, do you?'

'It certainly leaves a youngster high and dry, without much standing in the job market.'

'Oh, he's got a job, thank God, at a time when so many young people haven't.'

'What does he do?'

'He's in market research. Only knocking on people's doors, asking them what brand of detergent they use, or whether they like drinking lager. But a job's a job these days.'

'Do you think we might get down to business again, Mrs Toplady?'

The recording of her statement required patience on both sides. Beamish applied himself painstakingly and slowly. It gave him the opportunity to bring her mind back to the offences for which she might be charged. As one inexorable sentence after another went down on paper, she was becoming more and more convinced that she could not avoid an appearance in the dock.

I had no authority to enter the premises –

I know that I should have handed back the key when I left Mr Burgess's employ –

I did not take anything except the two dogs that belong to me –

I did open the doors of one or two rooms, just out of curiosity –

Beamish ceased to provide her with any crumb of hope or comfort, writing down her statement as a continuous prose answer to his ruthless leading questions. By the time she came to read the document before he let her sign it, she was a frightened woman again.

'It looks terrible, put down in black and white like this, Mr Beamish.'

Beamish let it be seen that he had no personal feelings in the matter.

'But that's how it happened, isn't it, Mrs Toplady? There's nothing you feel you want to add or change?'

'I only wish I'd gone nowhere near the house. I wish I'd never heard of the place.'

And when Beamish was about to leave, she seemed to fall under the compulsion to detain him. Although he was clearly likely to be the instrument of her downfall, there had grown up a personal relationship between them. It was as if she wanted to cling to him.

'Mr Beamish – when am I going to be able to speak to Mr Mosley?'

'That's hard for me to say, Mrs Toplady. Mr Mosley is a busy man. I don't know his exact programme, but he expects to be away from Bagshawe a good deal in the next few days.'

She sighed. It was the suspense that she could not bear, the waiting for vital decisions to be made by soulless strangers in cold, distant offices – days, perhaps even weeks hence.

'What you want to tell Mr Mosley, you could of course tell me,' Beamish said.

She could not make up her mind about this.

'I don't know whether –'

'I can pass anything on to Mr Mosley for you. I can always get a message to him, wherever he is.'

May God forgive him for such fantasy –

'I don't find it very easy,' Primrose Toplady said. 'You see, Mr Mosley already knows what it's about.'

'I've read the case-notes, Mrs Toplady. Mr Mosley always keeps me abreast of what's going on in his mind.'

By God, he was in inventive shape this morning! If he could only keep her teetering on the edge like this, she'd probably blurt out the beginnings of it involuntarily. Then the rest would follow. They had reached the front door. Beamish waited. Too much obvious persuasion at this stage, and she probably would wait until she could see Mosley.

'It seems so silly, when you look at it one way,' she said.

'I'd be very surprised if there was anything silly about it. Sometimes it clears one's mind, to talk to other people.'

'Have you the time, Mr Beamish? I promise I won't go on and on.'

They went back into the sitting-room. Mrs Toplady

fiddled nervously with a knitting stitch-counter that her fingers had encountered under her cushion.

'It's to do with why I left off working for Mr Burgess, Mr Beamish.'

'Yes. Mr Mosley did mention something about that.'

'I'm afraid I didn't tell Mr Mosley everything.'

'No?'

'Well, you see, the real reason seems so silly. You'll think I am out of my mind.'

'It's unlikely I'll think anything of the sort. You strike me as a woman very firmly in command of her mind.'

She looked very satisfied to hear that.

'But I wasn't firmly in command during the last few weeks before I left Garth, Mr Beamish. You see, the place had got so *weird*. The house was weird. Mr Burgess was behaving weirdly.' She halted, seemed not to know where it was best to go next.

'Of course, these old houses often do seem spooky,' Beamish said.

'I've never been one to fill my mind with that kind of thought – but Garth was never a nice house – so big, so cold and empty. There were so many rooms that no one ever went into from one year's end to the next. There were so many shadows, so many electric light bulbs missing. When you opened a door, you had the feeling that you did not know what you were going to find the other side of it. There were noises, too. The noises were the worst of all. Mice. Loose doors and windows. Bad plumbing. Timbers that creaked for no reason at all. And there were other sounds that there was no accounting for – sounds that you could not be really certain you had heard, because however hard you strained your ears, they didn't come again.'

'Of course, once you let that sort of thing start playing on your nerves –'

'Yes, but what really started to get me down was when I saw that something was getting on Mr Burgess's nerves too. He had never been bothered by anything like that all the time I had known him. He had never noticed anything weird about the house. It was a subject I'd never have dared to bring up in conversation with him: he'd have been down my throat in a second. The only things Mr Burgess had ever believed in in his life were things that he could see and count.'

'And then he started hearing things too?'

'He'd prick up his ears and make me listen.'

'And did you hear things?'

'Never so as to be sure about them – not those times when he'd heard something. Not to be absolutely sure.'

'What sort of things did he think he'd heard?'

'Voices, sometimes. People talking in other rooms. Music faint music.'

Faint music?

'Did you ever hear music yourself, Mrs Toplady?'

'No, I didn't. Not once. Except that when Mr Burgess was making me listen hard, I got into the state where I didn't know what I could hear and what I couldn't.'

'Did either of you ever go and look?'

'Often. I wasn't scared – not really scared – not scared, I mean, of going into rooms that I knew were empty. It wasn't that that frightened me. It was my *thoughts* that did that.'

Beamish considered.

'If this sort of thing was going on when you were in the house, Henry Burgess must have been getting himself pretty worked up when he was alone.'

'You could see what it was doing to him. He was losing weight. He would jump if a coal fell in the grate. I remember once he thought he heard someone talking in the breakfast room – a dark and damp little room that hadn't been used since Mrs Burgess's time. It was all making him shorter-tempered than usual. I couldn't stand it, Mr Beamish. I reached the stage where I couldn't stand another day of it. I told Mr Mosley that I left because of all the cycling across town in all weathers. But it wasn't that. Not only that, anyway. I couldn't stand to go into that house again.'

Now that she had come to the end of it, she did not seem as relieved as he would have expected her to be. She was still tense. Her colour was still high. She looked at Beamish, expecting some sort of support.

'You'll tell Mr Mosley all this?'

'The moment I see him. Mrs Toplady – do you think that

at this period, a little over two years ago, there was actually anyone living in Henry Burgess's house?'

'Only Mr Burgess.'

'I was thinking of squatters. Could anyone have managed to hide themselves in the house? Did you ever make a systematic search of the whole place?'

'We never did anything like that. It would never have crossed our minds. I don't believe that either of us seriously believed there was really anyone there. I don't believe that, even now. I don't see how there could have been. It was just the way the place was playing on our nerves.'

'And the way you were playing on each other's nerves, perhaps. But stranger things have been known to happen, Mrs Toplady. Did you ever find anything that might have suggested there was someone else on the premises?'

'Nothing like that.'

'Nothing in the dustbin that you or Henry Burgess hadn't put there yourselves?'

'I don't see how that could have happened.'

'Did you ever find any milk-bottles, for example, that hadn't been ordered either by you or Henry Burgess?'

Beamish saw the muscles in Primrose Toplady's cheeks tighten momentarily. The item had startled her – but she regained her self-control at once.

'No. I can't say that I remember anything of that nature.'

'Milk-bottles from a dairy in Ripon, Mrs Toplady. The Gledholt Dairy.'

'What would they be doing there?'

'I don't know, but Mr Mosley has evidence that empty bottles from the Gledholt Dairy were put out one morning for the milkman to collect.'

'Certainly that was nothing to do with me, and I never saw them. I can't for the life of me think how it could have happened. The milkman must have made a mistake.'

'Had Henry Burgess any connections with Ripon?'

'None that I know of.'

'If you recollect anything about these bottles, Mrs Toplady, you must let us know at once. And there is one more question to which I must have your clear answer. Why did you not tell the truth to Mr Mosley?'

'I did not want to look silly, Mr Beamish.'

When Beamish walked back through the town centre, there was an unusual sense of hush about the Market Place. It was not lack of noise: a mountain of canned peas was being unloaded by fork-lift at the supermarket with wholly disproportionate clatter. But the customary knot of idlers had retreated from the centre of the square. And that was because they were keeping their distance from Miley Morrison, who was sitting on the edge of the horse-trough in intense conversation with Mosley.

Beamish too withdrew from sight and indulged in a round of casual window-shopping. That was how he first came to take an active interest in Veronique's Boutique. There seemed to be an inordinate number of nubile females on the staff and, for a dress-shop, there was a remarkable traffic in and out of unaccompanied male customers.

Nine

When Mosley concluded his interview with Miles Morrison on the corner of the horse-trough, he walked away, paying no attention to those members of the leisured class who stood courteously aside for him to pass. Miley, on the other hand, remained sitting contemplatively, wearing the sort of smile that Leonardo da Vinci might have adorned him with if their paths had happened to cross.

Miley was disturbed by the way the dialogue had gone. Mosley had won every round on points, though Miley had flailed about himself with flamboyant abandon – and with righteousness. What put him in the Mona Lisa class was the smile he had had to assume to reassure his friends. He got up and walked with dignity to his command-spot, transmitting silent messages to a lieutenant here, a courier there, a fetcher of cigarettes over yonder.

Mosley had broken every police procedural rule that Miley knew about. Through a dense mesh of innuendo, he had made accusations for which he could not possibly possess proof: offences of which Miles was innocent. But Mosley had succeeded in conveying the meaning that he was a bastard who would stop at nothing if he was determined on a conviction. He claimed to know that Miley had handled wholesale quantities of canned pilchards in a layby. He knew of a liaison between Miley and a married woman on the Westlands Estate that he would happily bring to the notice of Miley's wife. He knew that Miley was responsible for criminal damage to an allotment shed belonging to a man who had fallen behind in payment of a bet he had lost on the outcome of a council by-election. He had gone on to make unveiled threats. Either Miley co-operated, and told Mosley what had been going on at Garth, or he was on his way up the river.

Miley found it incredible that an officer of Mosley's experience should leave himself so wide open to complaint. Not that Miley proposed laying any complaint: his imagination fell short of any pretext on which he might conceivably enter a police station of his own free will. Miley knew his rights and also reckoned to know his way about the new Police and Criminal Evidence Act. He tried to give Mosley a little elementary instruction in the same, but his efforts were feeble. They seemed feeble, even to himself. The only public image left to him was his enigmatic smile.

The Holgates lived in a red-brick villa up Buttergate Brow. Dickie had been able to purchase it (through Timothy John Fawcett) before it came officially on the market. Fawcett had in fact no great desire to be publicly associated with selling such a house. It was the sort of property that would have made a surveyor laugh, and that would have inspired little enthusiasm in the mortgage market. Any local government grant depended on so much fundamental work being done at the owner's expense, that Holgate had not bothered to ask for one. Webs of dry-rot extended under floorboards, water climbed out of the fountains from untraceable sources, paper peeled from the walls within a week of application. But Holgate was a brave man in the *Do It Yourself* context, and, what was even more to the point, his wife Avril shared his outlook. Neither was easily ruffled, and both believed that the present had to be endured to equip the future. One day Green Eaves would be a dream-house, saleable at a life-giving profit. Holgate bought scaffolding as a job lot in a bankruptcy sale. When he was in funds he bought bricks and worked Trojan-like at weekends. He borrowed a cement-mixer when he needed one, persuaded a heating engineer to teach him how to bend pipes.

The Holgates lived with this work going on around them,

and furnished the house on similar principles. Apart from their bed, Avril's sewing machine and Dickie's power drill, they looked upon little as their own. When they fancied any article that came into Dickie's hands by way of trade, they lived with it until they tired of it, or until they heard of a potential buyer. On one occasion a man called Hodgkins came without an appointment to buy and take away a refectory table (oak, repro) on which Avril was in the act of serving their lunch of tinned ravioli. A Georgian mahogany bowfront sideboard might serve for a month as a store for stone-ginger bottles and pewter tankards. A Victorian walnut serpentine three-tier whatnot might find itself cheek by jowl with an old mangle. On Friday nights Dickie would look over his stock to see what might prove irresistible on tomorrow's stall.

His stock was so miscellaneous, and in such a constant state of flux that he sometimes forgot what he owned. But today he was in the middle of a thorough stock-taking, going minutely over the shelves and through cupboards, comparing their contents with the police lists. By now he was actually hoping to find something iniquitous – something to take to Mosley with a spectacular display of frankness. Avril was in similar mood: she went upstairs and came back with a pair of brass candlesticks in the shape of Corinthian pillars, a framed print of a flower study by Van Husen and six silver coffee spoons in a case.

'All bought from the same man,' she said. 'I trust you're not going to protect him.'

'Not on your life.'

'Promise –'

'No need to make me.'

Avril was attractive in an essentially *negligee* fashion. She tended to dress as she furnished her home. She never lacked boldly contrasting colours.

'I've got to find him first,' Dickie said.

'Don't try to take that on yourself. Go and see Inspector Mosley now. Don't waste time.'

'Give me ten minutes with the man. Somebody ought to try to talk some sense into him.'

Dickie took off his stubble with a three-headed Philishave

destined for the stall at the weekend, discarded the sweat-shirt he was wearing (*Hi, Sexy-eyes!*) and replaced it with one that proclaimed him an alumnus of Princeton.

He found Primrose Toplady at home, still limp from her encounter with Sergeant Beamish, and blinking out across her garden path as if she had no reason to expect pleasure from any caller. She recognized Dickie. She had seen him on the market – though she would certainly never have patronized his stall; you had to be either wealthier or poorer than the Topladys to do that.

'It's no use you coming here –'

She evidently thought he was buying junk from door to door.

'If I might just have a moment of your time, Mrs Toplady – if you could tell me how I might get in touch with your Kevin –'

'I shall tell you nothing of the kind.'

Dickie was not entirely at a loss to account for this vehemence. Kevin's mother undoubtedly looked on general dealers as bad company. The door closed on him – and he lacked Sergeant Beamish's skill with his foot. A woman watched him knowledgeably over a back-garden fence as he came away. He knew that if Avril had been with him she would have propelled him at once in the direction of the police station. He still wanted, however, to have a word with Kevin Toplady first.

Not all the pupils at St Christopher's select private school at Bradburn were as scrubbed and exclusive as Janet Morrison and her friend Sarah Wainwright, who were as inseparable as was permitted by the ten awkward miles between their home villages. (Sarah lived at Upper Akehurst, a settlement so isolated that it was a standing joke in both Bradburn and Bagshawe.)

Some girls squashed their hats into their satchels or sports-bags within yards of leaving the school gates. There was a *Ladies* in the bus-station that lent itself ideally to the application of cosmetics – even in certain advanced cases to a change from school uniform to jeans: there were boys at a neighbouring comprehensive who were sensitive to the outward signs of social distinction. But for various reasons, not entirely straightforward, Janet and Sarah preferred to abide by the rules. They sat daily for an hour on a wooden bench in the bus-station.

'God!' Janet said. 'She's set sodding quadratics again.'

'Christ Almighty!'

'I can't get the hang of those bloody factors. That means using the bloody formula. You do the odd buggers, and I'll do the even bastards. That will save half the time.'

They were working with their exercise books balanced on their knees when a young woman came along, scanning the faces of St Christopher girls in the bus queues. She was a soiled brunette in her twenties, and had difficulty peering through a curtain of hair.

'Does anyone know a girl called Janet Morrison?'

'She's looking for you, Janet.'

Some busybody from 4B pointed out where Janet was sitting.

'Are you Janet Morrison?'

'Who wants to know?'

'From 28, Holland Row?'

'What's that got to do with you?'

'I've a message from your Mum. She's gone over to do for your Auntie Eunice, over in Hadley Dale. She's had a funny turn.'

'And what am I supposed to do about it?'

'It's what I'm supposed to do. Your Mum asked me to take you over to Hadley. Your uncle will run you both home when he comes in from work.'

'Shit! And who are you?'

'You wouldn't know me. I'm staying with my sister in Lake Villas. Mrs Redfern.'

'Never heard of her.'

'Are you coming, then?'

Janet left Sarah applying the formula to odd and even problems alike.

Miley was at first irritable, then visibly nervous, then

66

positively frightened. He left the house and went to the Market Place, which in the evening became a different kind of HQ: for young men doing wheelies on their Hondas. Miley went straight to the telephone-booth, where he rang the bus-station and had difficulty in making the nature of his enquiry clear. Even when he succeeded, they gave him no sort of useful answer. So he rang the Bradburn bus office, at the far end of the route – but gave up after five minutes of the ringing tone.

There was nothing for it, then, but to break the rule of a life-time and walk voluntarily into the police station, where he failed in his attempt to insist on dealing only with Mosley. A phlegmatic desk-sergeant eventually organized a statement from him – and then did contact Mosley on an internal line.

Ten

It was an evening of precarious domestic balance in at least three families in Bagshawe Broome. Miles Morrison was even uncertain about going out for his usual six pints, so unwilling was he to be away from home in case the scuffers had news for him. His wife was darning, and whatever fermentation might be going on inside her, she succeeded in maintaining a coolly controlled exterior. It riled her husband more than a session of nervous nagging would have done. He sought in vain for some rationalization for blaming her for their daughter's disappearance but had to content himself with informing her that she did not care. This broke the dam and the flood-waters of years of suppression broke through. She told Miles truths about himself that no man of his quality could bear to hear, and for a tottering second it looked as if he was going to strike her. Instead, he strode out for the Lansdowne, ordering her, under threat of maiming, to come and fetch him if there were any messages.

Differences of opinion were not unknown in the Holgate household, but the sun rarely went down on them. Dickie and Avril were both too naturally easy-going to keep a quarrel up for long. The trouble tonight was that Avril had found out – pretty easily, because Dickie was fairly transparent – that he had not been to see Mosley yet.

'You really think you're going to deal with this on your own? Where are you going to start looking for him?'

'He must be in the neighbourhood somewhere.'

'And if you find him – what next?'

Dickie was not articulate about it. Did he in fact know?

'I shall talk to him.'

'Talk to him? What about?'

'I don't know. Find out what's got into him. Try to persuade him to talk honestly to Mosley.'

'Isn't that his problem? You'll have problems of your own if you start playing games with Mosley. What's all this about, Dickie: some sort of schoolboy honour?'

'I've known him since we were both nippers.'

'And that puts you under an obligation? To risk your reputation and our living?'

'It isn't quite like that.'

'What is it like, then? Kevin Toplady's a criminal, and Mosley thinks you might be too.'

'I haven't said I'm not going to see Mosley.'

'Go now, then. Give him a ring.'

'It would be better to speak to him personally.'

'Well – he isn't here, is he?'

And then something in Avril Holgate fractured. Her outburst was like nothing that Dickie had ever witnessed from her before. Up to now he would have said that their relationship was as exemplary as a young marriage in the late twentieth century could be. Now it suddenly seemed as if she had been building up resentment since the first morning of their honeymoon.

'You're too soft. You're too gutless. You haven't even the staying power to hype a price up when you've something on your hands worth selling. What hold has Kevin Toplady got over you? When we were desperate to move in here, you kept giving them another day, another twelve hours. And that woman he had in tow: they thought they were the Bonnie and Clyde of Bagshawe Broome.'

They didn't break into any banks. They didn't kill anybody – but Dickie thought better of saying it.

'Either,' she said, 'you go here and now and tell Inspector Mosley everything you know about that couple, or –'

'Or what?'

But she hesitated to say it.

'Or what?' he dared to repeat.

'Or we shall have to take a good look at how things are

69

between us. I'm not going to live on the brink of this sort of thing. Either we are straight and are seen to be straight, or –'

'Have I ever been otherwise?'

'You've acted otherwise – whenever Kevin Toplady's been concerned. That's why I ask: what do you owe him?'

'I suppose I'm sorry for him. He's so inadequate.'

'He's had a better chance than many in Bagshawe to make himself adequate.'

'There could be more than one opinion about that.'

'So you're still his protector? If you won't go to see Mr Mosley, I shall.'

'There's no need for that. I'll go now.'

'We'll both go.'

A similar decision was reached by a different thought-process in the Toplady home. The thought-processing was done by Primrose.

'Father –' she said, and when she called Kitchener *father*, he always knew there was something solemn and fateful in the offing.

'Father, I've been thinking.'

Kitchener blinked, and wished that the impending scene was not going to take place, that some unforeseen caller at their door would postpone the palaver. But the door-bell remained unhelpfully silent.

'About this business at Garth, and this Inspector Mosley –'

The use of *this* to qualify Mosley was in itself a subtle signal. It put Mosley at a short, artificially created distance, at the same time as acknowledging that he could not be entirely discounted.

'About our Kevin, you mean?'

'Who else would it be about, but our Kevin?'

Kitchener was moodily silent, weighing up the possibilities.

'It needs a bit of thought,' he said at last.

'That's the last thing on earth that it needs. We can go on being tight-lipped, but they'll still get to know. That Inspector Mosley is like a cat watching a mousehole. He'll stay there, twitching his tail day and night. And that young sergeant who came this morning was as sharp as a bee-sting, and twice as barbed.'

'You know what it will mean,' Kitchener said.

'It will mean something worse if we go on like this. They'll think we've something to hide.'

'Well, we have, haven't we?'

His wife looked at him with three times the barbs of Sergeant Beamish. It was no part of his role to make that kind of pronouncement, true though it might be.

'It's no use rushing at things, mother.'

'I don't want to find myself up in court at my age.'

'It'll not come to that, mother.'

'Once these people get their teeth into you, they'll stop at nothing. I should never be able to hold my head up in Bagshawe Broome again.'

'I don't see what they can say we've done.'

'That Mr Mosley was talking about me obstructing him.'

'Nay, mother – all we've ever done is to protect our own.'

'And be let down for it.'

She started to cry. Only four other five times in her married life had she ever cried.

'So you'd better make your mind up,' she said.

'You mean, what we're going to tell them?'

'We're going to tell them everything,' she said. 'Everything they need to know, anyway.'

'I'll turn it over in my mind.'

'You'll do no such thing. You'll go upstairs and get yourself changed this minute. We'll strike while we're in the mood. And there's another thing: when we do get to the police station, I don't want to sit there doing all the talking, same as usually happens. He's your son as well as mine. And don't put that shirt on you wore last Saturday. It has tobacco-burns down the front.'

As they left the house, she suggested turning left and taking the footpath between their estate and the top end of town.

'That way we shan't have every Tom, Dick and Harry working out where we're going and why.'

Mosley was in the middle of a less than reasonable interview with Miley when the first of his other callers was announced.

Miley was moving unpredictably from phase to phase of drunkenness. One minute he was maudlin with affection for his saintly Janet, the next he was cursing the ineptitude of a Force that had not brought her back yet. Then he was forecasting the violence that he would perform on her abductor when his identity became known. Then, remembering his humiliation in the Market Square this morning, he turned his vehemence on Mosley.

Mosley did not take offence. The last thing he wanted to do was to have to take official cognizance of the state that Miley was in. Miley's bellicosity dissolved. He laid a muscular arm round Mosley's neck and leaned his seventeen stone on Mosley's shoulders. Mosley had difficulty in remaining upright.

'Besh bugger I could have on the job. Besh bugger from Hadley Dale to Bradcaster. Every bugger shays sho. "If Jack Moshley can't find her, can't be found." Tell you wha', Mr Moshley: you get that bugger, and before you shlam him in, give me five minish with him.'

He moved the crook of his elbow, so that his weight shifted and all but brought Mosley down.

'Now look, Miley,' Mosley told him. 'Don't you think it's time you went home? Sergeant Beamish will drive you.'

'I'm staying here, Mr Mosley, till something comes through.'

'That's a bad idea, Miley. We'll send a squad car for you if anything crops up.'

Not many months ago, Beamish would not have regarded the safe-conduct home of a drunken lout as an appropriate use of his talents. But sorties under Mosley's oblique and sometimes grotesque tutelage had taught him to take pride in the diversity of chores to which he could apply himself. The trouble was that Miley's volatility of spirit was such that no consistent strategy worked. Miley seemed to cotton on to the idea at first, even to take to Beamish. As they left the police station, a wave of sweating bonhomie took possession of him. Beamish controlled his reeling motion by the varying pressure of an elbow. As they crossed the front office, his

72

attitude to the constabulary was in one of its upswings. He took an admiring interest in such incidents of professional activity as he recognized *en passant*. He smiled benignly on the efforts of a sergeant to explain to a motorist the consequences of refusing to give a specimen. He greeted a young man who had just been brought in with a consignment of stolen jam in catering-size tins.

Beamish steered him across the transport-yard, and once he was in the passenger-seat, Miley went into a state of serene coma. But as they were turning right at the Lansbury Street lights, they had to brake suddenly for a Mini that was trying to beat the amber. The whiplash was enough to wake Miley, who was alarmed to find himself in a strange car, askew and stationary in the middle of a crossroads. He had forgotten who Beamish was and put into operation at once his belief in attack as the best means of defence. Beamish completed his right turn and parked by a convenient strip of nearside pavement.

'Now listen, Morrison – get hold of yourself. You may not be able to remember much of this evening, but try to put some of it together. You've been to see Inspector Mosley of your own free will, and I'm taking you home.'

'You a scuffer? What's the bloody law coming to?'

'Your daughter's missing – remember? We've got every stop out, and every manual coupled. I'm taking you home, because that's where a ransom note is most likely to arrive.'

There were people in Miley's front room who, Beamish could see, were not accustomed to be there. He recognized faces from the Market Square – staff officers of Miley's. There were not many of them – in fact, only two – but they appeared to fill the room – and for some reason, Miley took virulent exception to their presence. They had been to the Lansdowne to tell him something, and not finding him there had decided to come and tell his wife. It was an act of derring-do: Miley did not encourage visits to the privacy of his home. He glowered at them with incredulous rage.

'These gentlemen have something to tell you, Miles,' his frail and pallid wife said.

This convinced Miley that she was in treacherous collusion with them. He took an aggressive half-step towards them,

73

and one of them sidestepped so adroitly that he almost knocked his wife down.

Half an hour later, Beamish arrived back at the police station with Miley handcuffed to his wrist. He announced to the desk-sergeant that he proposed to charge him, and that in the meanwhile he should be kept in custody, deprived of his bootlaces, belt and braces, and anything else with which he might damage himself or anyone who came into his bilious field of vision.

Eleven

Mosley was outraged when it was reported to him what Beamish had done. He rushed downstairs and with blood-shot eyes ordered the station sergeant to refuse to accept any charge against Miley.

'What do you think the press will make of this – arresting a man who's beside himself with grief and anxiety?'

'It wasn't safe to leave him alone with his wife,' Beamish said.

'That was the only safe thing to do. Emily Morrison would have known how to handle him. She does it seven nights week.'

Beamish was visibly abashed at the rebuke, but Mosley did not relent.

'Unnecessary paperwork and a bad reputation with every informant in the district – that's what you'll get for arresting Miley. And now, if you can tear yourself away from him, do you feel like doing any useful work this evening?'

'There are one or two things you ought to know – things that two men came to his house to tell him. There were people who saw Janet Morrison leave on the Bradburn bus this morning.'

'Very clever of them. She does that every morning.'

'And they recognized other people on the bus.'

'The same people have travelled daily on that bus since Noah and Japheth,' Mosley said.

'Yes. But there were two this morning who aren't usually on it – who aren't often seen in Bagshawe Broome. Couple

75

of hippies, one with a pair of nail-scissors hanging from the lobe of one ear. And he had a woman with him with hair all over her face. They didn't know her, but people are pretty sure who he was.'

'And how much longer are you going to keep me waiting for the dramatic climax?'

'Kevin Toplady with female escort.'

'And what's news about that?'

'They were looking at Janet Morrison.'

'Oh, aye? And don't people look at her as a rule, then? Is she a sight from which bus-travellers usually avert their eyes?'

'These friends of Morrison's said they were looking at her very curiously – talking about her – in a peculiar way. Secretive.'

Mosley grunted.

'Then when they got off the bus, they seemed to be following the girl – as if they wanted to know where her school was.'

'And this has enabled you to formulate some theory, has it, Sergeant Beamish?'

'I think it might be worth following up, sir.'

'Follow it up, then. And in the meanwhile, there's a couple waiting somewhere about the station to see me. I've got my hands full with a pair of beauties of my own. See what this other pair want.'

Mosley turned away, then looked back.

'And I doubt if there's any call to arrest the buggers.'

Mosley stumped away into the bare-walled interview room, where the Topladys were waiting, straight-backed and comfortless, for the continuation of a dialogue that they were wishing they had never initiated.

'Some interesting titbits are coming to light, one at a time,' Mosley said.

If he had been unusually short with Beamish, he was being continuously spiteful with the Topladys.

'You didn't tell me that your Kevin has been in Bagshawe Broome in the last twenty-four hours.'

'We didn't know he had,' Primrose Toplady snapped back. And Kitchener, who in spite of her injunction, had scarcely been able to contribute a word, made a pathetic attempt to enter the conversation, with something of the appeal of a reprimanded spaniel.

'Inspector – you can't hold us responsible for what he does. He's passed the stage where we can account for him.'

'That's as may be, but you've not passed the stage of telling lies to stop the neighbours from talking, have you? I'm going to do it,' Mosley said. 'I'm going to do what I said I would: something I've never done to man, woman or child in my working life. I'm going to do you two for wasting police time.'

Lightning had been flashing in his eyes, but they suddenly withdrew into their sockets with a lustreless intensity. While he had been out of the room, the Topladys had evidently conferred. They were utterly incapable of handling the situation as he had stirred it up.

'Look, Mr Mosley – if only you'd let us begin at the beginning and tell it in our own way –'

Primrose Toplady's eyes were bulbous in desperate appeal.

'It seems to me you've begun at the beginning fifteen times already and we've still not got as far as the middle of the story.'

'If only you let us *talk*, Mr Mosley.'

'You seem to have done nothing else since you came into this room. Why not let your husband have a go for a change?'

Kitchener looked as if the interview was having the worst possible effects on his gastric.

'I only wish he would talk, instead of sitting there looking like Guy Fawkes.'

She promptly closed her mouth with dramatic finality, her lips becoming a long, straight, narrow slit out of which all colour had been pressed. Kitchener blew out his cheeks to suppress a gastric manifestation.

'Looks as if she's giving you the go-ahead,' Mosley told him.

'It's hard for us, you know, Mr Mosley. We can't think where we've gone wrong.'

Mosley looked at him for some seconds with sad appraisal.

'Perhaps it hasn't occurred to you that you haven't gone wrong,' he said at last.

They were the first conciliatory words he had spoken in an hour and a half, but they were far from trusting him by now.

'We've made our Kevin what he was,' Kitchener Toplady said.

'No. God did that.'

It was unexpected. Toplady eased his bottom in his chair. His wife did not yet relax her lips, but she began to look as if that possibility might exist.

'That's not how we look at things,' Toplady said. 'That would be sheltering.'

Mosley muttered something that neither of the Topladys could make out.

'I didn't quite catch what you said, Mr Mosley.'

'I said that I don't see why a couple shouldn't shelter. It depends what you're sheltering from. Are you sheltering from facts that you can't avoid – or are you sheltering from what Bagshawe Broome might say about them?'

'All along, we've only wanted to do what's right. We've never treated Kevin any different from any of the others.'

'So what if he *is* different from the others?'

Kitchener Toplady wriggled.

'Right's right and wrong's wrong. Every one of the others has been a credit to us. Eric's head of his department and next in line to be deputy headmaster. They think the world of Charles in his physics department. His professor has told him that his thesis on wave motion could become the basis of an international textbook.'

'I know. Everybody keeps telling me all this. You've every reason to be proud. But none of that is a substitute for telling me the truth about Kevin.'

'Mother told you the truth.'

'No. She didn't. She waltzed all round it, trying to hide it from herself.'

'You don't make things any easier by getting on at us, Mr Mosley.'

'Well, I'm not getting on at you at the moment – I'm doing my best to see things how you see them. And I've come to a new conclusion,' Mosley said.

78

Kitchener looked at him hopefully. Primrose let her mouth relax at last.

'I've come to the conclusion that you haven't told me the whole truth because you don't really know it. You don't know it, because you won't let yourself know it. And in any case, you're too near to it to understand it.'

'If only we could have our time over again.'

'Well, you can't, Mrs Toplady. But are you going to try to help me get at the truth?'

'We won't try to hide anything, Mr Mosley.'

'If you do, it's from yourself that you're hiding it,' Mosley said. 'And on the whole, I'd still prefer your husband to do most of the talking, from now on.'

It was not a return to his previous irascibility, but the promise was writ hugely that any relapse would be irreversible.

'Mother didn't tell me at first,' Kitchener said. 'She didn't tell me for days. I couldn't make out what was wrong with her. I could see she had something on her mind. You see, she'd heard this rattling, out in Henry Burgess's kitchen –'

In the other room, Beamish knew he was not doing well. He was not fully concentrating. He was still smarting from the slapping down he had had from Mosley. His relationship with the Inspector had always been an eccentric one, it was true – everything to do with Mosley was at least slightly off beam. But it had also been one of the most richly formative factors in Beamish's maturing. Beamish would always be in the forefront in admitting that, but it was difficult to see how their friendship, even a working understanding, was going to survive this recent onslaught. It was so unregardful of fact, so unfair. And sitting at the table in front of Beamish, not exactly nervous, but with a sense of one-off occasion, were the Holgates, who had quite obviously come after much heart- and future-searching. He could see that Dickie Holgate was tense. At his side, his wife had the makings of a good-looking woman – but her looks were playing second fiddle to her state of mind. Avril Holgate's eyes were glistening with the determination behind a recent decision –

and with the stubbornness to see it through. Beamish told himself — without strong conviction — that what was a comparative non-event for him, a routine interview in a difficult but scarcely top-line case, was something unique for this pair. It behoved him to treat them as unique.

'You have something to tell me, I believe. Which of you is going to start us off?'

Avril did not flash a signal to Dickie, nor did she play about with embarrassed introductory passages. Dickie went straight into the meat of the story.

'When Avril and I bought our house — that was between two and three years ago — it was in a disgusting state.'

His wife looked as if she might have had something bitter to say, but she disciplined herself.

'We also had squatters. Kevin Toplady: does that name mean anything to you?'

'You can assume that I've heard it. We can mop up any secondary questions later.'

'Kevin Toplady and his girlfriend, Bootsie Bateman. Maybe it would be better if we left her till later, too. Let's get the main facts first. They were living in infinitely worse conditions than we would have put up with at our lowest ebb.'

'Believe it or not,' Avril could not restrain herself from muttering.

'They asked for time, in the first instance a week, to look for somewhere else to set up their sticks.'

'Their sticks? They were able to carry away their entire possessions in a couple of dustbin-liners,' Avril said.

'I gave them that week. They even offered to pay me rent — not in money, but in kind.'

Holgate opened a sports-bag he had brought with him and produced a stoppered decanter and a carved ivory medallion.

'And there were one or two other things that I'm afraid I've already sold. I'll admit that I've not always been very careful about going over your official lists. That was not dishonesty. I'll ask you to believe it was sheer lack of time.'

'I shall still want the details, before we've finished.'

'To cut a long story as short as I can, he pleaded for more

80

time, another half a week, then a couple of days and finally, after the last twenty-four-hour postponement, I practically threw them out. They weren't ideal lodgers.'

'Dickie,' Avril said, 'has a very kind heart – where Kevin Toplady is concerned.'

'This is a point on which Avril and I have always differed. It isn't that Kevin and I have ever been friends, far from it, but there's always been something about him that – well, it's difficult to explain.'

'Very,' from Avril.

'Something fascinating – more than that. Something you had to admire.'

'Christ!' from between his wife's clenched teeth. Without seeming spectacularly rude, Dickie ignored her.

'He was his own man. He was so outstandingly his own man that you had to respect him for it. When we were at school, Upper Peel Street, he'd be about fifteen and I'd be three classes lower, but everybody knew Kevin Toplady. I remember once the headmaster caned him in front of the whole school – he was the sort who still did that kind of thing. You could see old Weightman taking aim on the palm of Kevin's hand, cut and come again, determined to make it hurt, and make Kevin show he'd been hurt. And Kevin was equally determined to show nothing.'

Avril Holgate's face was that of a woman wondering how many more repetitions of that story she could stand.

'Who won?' Beamish asked.

'Kevin came down from the platform smirking.'

'You haven't told us what he'd done to deserve it,' Avril said.

'That's entirely beside the point. It doesn't matter. It was Kevin Toplady against the System – as it always was Kevin Toplady against the System – because the System was always against him.'

'You'll have Sergeant Beamish wondering what we've come to tell him,' Avril said.

'This all has to do with what we're here to tell you, Sergeant Beamish, because it's only fair to me for you to know my attitude to Kevin Toplady. I don't know how much you know about the Topladys. To call them toffee-nosed is not doing them justice. They've got brains. They work as if their greatest ambition is to run their own sweat-shop. Whatever trees they climb, they get to the top. Their Eric is on his way to becoming a headmaster before he's forty. Their Charles has his knapsack bulging with whatever wand of office university professors have. Their Grace is practically executive manager of a symphony orchestra. All out of a two-and-a-half-bedroomed semi on the East Ward Estate. And all except Kevin, who never did fit in – maybe because nobody ever asked him what he wanted. Nobody knows what niche they had in mind for Kevin. It's always been said that it's Primrose Toplady's secret sorrow that none of her brood went for medicine or the law. They had their kids for their own glorification, did the Topladys, that's the whole truth of it. But Kevin didn't want to know.'

'Perhaps from the first day he could walk he was on the look out for somebody like Bootsie Bateman,' Avril said.

'Let's be honest. He was in trouble before Bootsie Bateman came into his life. When he was about thirteen there was something about shoplifting from Woolworth's, and Kevin landed in the juvenile court. His mother briefed a barrister to defend him – no mere Bagshawe solicitor for her boy. She spent her tea-caddy savings on a wig and gown from Manchester. He got the lad off on some smart technicality which, I don't need to tell you, did him no good at all.'

'Had he any ability?'

'I'm not sure whether Kevin has a brain or not. I strongly suspect he could match any of the Topladys, but he's always been damned if he'd use his ability the way they wanted. He's basically lazy too, and that's something that's been reinforced by habit.'

'And Bootsie Bateman.'

'And now I'll come to the nitty-gritty. Kevin gave me some bits and pieces in payment of token rent. He's also sold me the odd trinket from time to time, when he's been broke. And I've accepted them, without as much thought as I ought to have given it. But there were one or two things, as Inspector Mosley is well aware, that came from Henry Burgess's. I'm not making any accusation. This isn't even hearsay. But if I were you and the inspector, I'd be walking all round the possibility that Kevin and Bootsie spent some time squatting in Garth: while his mother was working there. That was how Kevin knew how to twist the knife. Maybe they squatted in other houses too.'

'Now tell me something about this young Bateman lady,' Beamish said.

'There was this rattling about in the kitchen,' Toplady said.

'And you have to give mother her due: she has nerves like steel cabling. You wouldn't have caught me going into that kitchen without a poker in my hand.'

'Once when we thought we had a burglar at home, I was first downstairs,' Mrs Toplady said.

'Mother was in there in a stride –'

'As I had been darting about the house a dozen times within that last week, chasing noises, real and imaginary.'

'And who did she find there but, I am ashamed to say, our Kevin treating the place as if it were his own. And that young woman. And, I am further ashamed to say, both of them drunk, out of an enamel mug, with a bottle of spirits on the table. Mother thought at first they had come in to see her, knowing her working hours, and that they were simply making themselves free of Henry Burgess's property for the morning. But she gradually put it together, from one thing or another, that they had been there several days. At first they had taken possession of one of the empty upstairs rooms and only used the kitchen after Mr Burgess had gone to bed. But then they found that him being as deaf and infirm as he was, they could take chances. They started living cheekily. It makes my blood run cold. I blame the woman entirely. I think they must have begun to look on it as some sort of game, leaving things until the last minute, shutting one door of a room the moment he opened the other. Playing loud music, then dashing into some other part of the house with their portable stereo.'

'Anything more unlike the Kevin we used to know, I can't imagine. He'd never have done anything like that before he met that girl. Of course, Mr Burgess did catch them in the end. They must have got careless, or else they were so full of drink that they didn't know what they were doing.'

'I can't think why Mr Burgess didn't go to the police. I can only think that they must have threatened him, terrified him, told him what they would do to him.'

And this was at the time when the old man was still turning out for his daily sandwich at Bert Hardcastle's, less willing than ever to talk to anyone. In fear of a broken skull?

'Neither of you thought of coming to the police yourselves?' Mosley asked them.

'Mr Mosley – he was our son.'

'I know that, Mrs Toplady. Don't you think it would have been better for him in the long run if –'

'Mr Mosley – I told him what sort of trouble he'd find himself in. I left him in no doubt about that.'

'And you gave up working at Garth?'

'What would you expect me to do?'

'Where do the two china dogs enter into the story?'

'Mr Burgess had them on his kitchen mantelpiece. I told you about them. One day, when I was trying to get on with my work, Kevin was capering about, showing off, and I told him to be careful, or he'd knock one of them down. I should have kept my mouth closed, because of course he picked them up one at a time and smashed them on the floor. That was why I bought a pair and put them in place of the others.'

'Tell me what you know about Miss Bateman.'

The question was out of their reach. To them Bootsie was irretrievably bad. They gaped at the suggestion that anyone could think otherwise.

'She's evil, that's what she is,' Primrose Toplady said. '"He that toucheth pitch shall be defiled therewith".'

'What sort of things does she talk about?' Mosley asked.

'How should we know what she talks about?'

'You've not ever invited her to your home?'

Primrose Toplady performed an interesting paradox, theoretically impossible. She both cringed and drew herself haughtily together in the same movement.

'Mr Mosley! What sort of people do you take us for?'

'Mindless sex,' Avril Holgate said. 'When they're not

working up to it for all to see, they're getting over the last bout. They think about nothing else. They talk about nothing else, in a sneering, secret-code sort of way. And they seem to think that everybody else conducts their lives along the same lines. And when their vibes, as they call them, are in the doldrums, then they can't stand the sight of each other. Then they're Kilkenny cats, spitting and clawing. I don't know how many times they've split up – but up to now they've always come together again.'

'Drugs?' Beamish asked.

'I wouldn't be surprised. They're into everything that's unclean and self-destructive.'

'That isn't fair, Avril,' Holgate said. 'I don't doubt Kevin's smoked grass in his time, when he was at the Technical College. So did I, for that matter, when I was that age – once. I take it for granted that they've both been on at least one hard trip, but that would only be experiment. The stuff's there. The experience might be interesting. I can't imagine they've never tried it. But during the time we knew them, and whenever I've caught sight of them since, I've seen none of the classical signs. I've never seen them in junkie company. Alcohol, yes – a good deal too much of it – but even that's more than they can usually afford. I mean, it looks to me very much as if their criminal activities would be hardly enough to pay for their groceries. But they know more about the small print of their social security entitlements than the girl behind the DHSS counter does. And it seems to me that it's when they're running out of vodka that they look round for something to knock off.'

'And you've always leaned over backwards to keep him out of trouble,' Avril said.

'Because one lot of trouble could only plunge him deeper into more. As for the times they've split up – what happens when they do? They wander about like lost souls, looking for each other, because even if it's nothing but in-fighting when they're together, they like life even less when they're apart. They give each other something, even if it's something that wouldn't do for Avril and me.'

Then Mosley entered the room, looking contented and affable, and showing no trace of his recent dissatisfaction with Beamish. He came round to Beamish's side of the table, picked up and glanced casually at Beamish's notes.

'I asked someone else this question just now, and got no sort of an answer. What sort of things does Miss Bateman talk about?'

'Sex,' Avril Holgate said. 'Every variation of it. Ad nauseam.'

'Other things, too,' Dickie corrected. 'Bootsie has three A levels. But only two Grade As. She was a little too experimental, she said, with Keats's *Hyperion*, and that brought her Eng Lit mark down to a B.'

'So she outclasses Kevin Toplady?'

'By a mile and a half. I don't know how many O levels Kevin got – one, I think: woodwork. He went to the Tech when he left school to try to do running repairs – but he did less work there than he'd done in Upper Peel Street. He's had jobs, market research once, door-to-door. That lasted a week.'

'You'd say she was a cut above the Toplady lad socially, too?'

'The sort of distance you'd need seven-league boots to cover,' Dickie said. 'That to me has always been the oddest thing about the partnership.'

'Who is she, then? And where's she from?'

'She talks as if her father is some sort of professional man, but I've never heard her say precisely what. She talks as if she can't stand him or her mother. Her home's somewhere in Yorkshire, north of here. Pontefract, Selby or Ripon – somewhere like that.'

'Ripon? That's where the milk bottles came from. It looks as if she sometimes brought her own milk to Garth, then. Have you anything else to tell us, young man?'

'Only about these one or two things that I'd have handed over months ago if I'd been wider awake,' Holgate said, and showed Mosley the things he had given to Beamish. Mosley did not need to look at them closely.

'Better check to make sure – but I think we shall find these connect with Soulgate Manor and Lytham.'

The Holgates were dismissed. The Topladys had already gone. 'The next thing will be the ransom note,' Mosley said.

'But I don't expect anything in that line before tomorrow morning. In the meanwhile, we'd better be looking for house property that has recently become unoccupied.'

'It's beginning to look as if that's their regular pattern,' Beamish said.

Mosley looked at his watch.

'It's not too late to ring Timothy John Fawcett at home. He knows everything that's on the market – and not just what's going through his own office.'

He made a move towards the phone.

'There's just one thing, sir,' Beamish said. 'Are we friends again now?'

Mosley looked at him uncomprehending.

'You gave me a rough time, earlier this evening, Mr Mosley.'

'Oh – that!'

Mosley shoved it to one side without embarrassment.

'I had to take it out of the Topladys. Just had to level them flat before I could make a proper start, and with me it's all or nothing. If I have to act bad-tempered, I have to be bad-tempered.'

Twelve

'What are we going up here for? This isn't the way to Hadley Dale.'

'We've got another call to make first,' Bootsie told her. They were driving towards Hempshaw End.

'My mum'll have gone home from my Auntie Eunice's by the time we get there,' Janet Morrison said.

She had so far showed no fear, but looked querulously critical. She was sitting with Bootsie on the broken springs of the back seat of the brown battered car that had at one time been parked on the edge of the Westlands Estate. In places the upholstery had been torn away and the window-ledge behind them was littered with felt mascots, grease-sodden takeaway cartons and screwed-up potato crisp packets. Under their feet there were dry leaves, sand, pebbles and Pay-and-Display parking tickets. Janet Morrison had not commented on any of this. The look on her shining scrubbed face was such as had no need for recourse to words. There was a conscious superiority about her that spoke for itself.

Kevin Toplady steered them up an unmade road between two fields, that did not look as if they were usable for anything.

'This doesn't go anywhere,' Janet said.

'It's time to put the blinkers on the kid,' Kevin said.

Bootsie drew out from under herself a musty old blanket and threw it over the girl's head, pulling a corner of it down under her buttocks and knotting two corners over her thighs. Janet struggled violently, which had the unreasonable effect

88

of making Bootsie angry with her. Bootsie had been up to now very civil, even convincingly friendly to the child. But now that she had a sacked octopus on her hands, she applied the force necessary to subdue it. In the wrestling bout that was involved, her hair fell even more wildly than usual about her face, making her a fair match for a schoolgirl knotted into a blanket. There was an ominous sound of bone meeting resistance as Janet's head knocked against what had once been an arm-rest and for nearly twenty seconds there was a worrying silence.

'Oh, Christ!' Bootsie said to herself.

Then Janet spoke with foul blanket stuffed into her mouth.

'Tell her to stow it,' Kevin shouted.

'Not to worry, Kev. She's stowed.'

Yet when Bootsie came to untruss her at their journey's end, Janet was still remarkably undishevelled – or, at least, she seemed able to restore herself to normality with no more than a shake of her shoulders. She was red in the face, it was true, but her high forehead still glistened. She picked off an inch of thread here, tweezed away a bit of fluff there, put her hand up behind her pig-tails, wriggled inside her clothes – and was almost as immaculate as she was at her bus-stop.

'What have we come to this effing hole for?' she asked.

'That's no way to talk,' Bootsie said. 'Swear if you want to. But if you're scared of saying the words, don't try to sound big.'

Kevin had gone on ahead to wrestle with a doorlock.

'For Christ's sake get her into this shit-ridden house,' he said.

'Don't you bloody start. I was hoping this was going to be a civilized party for a change. Let's keep it clean, shall we?'

'Oh, Christ!'

'What now?'

'The bloody key's broken.'

'I told you to get another cut. You could see it was cracked nearly through.'

'We'll have to break a back window.'

'Go and do it, then. And don't wake the neighbourhood.'

Which was silly, because there did not seem to be another house in sight. Dusk was advanced. Kevin stumbled over rubbish as he made his way down the side of the house. It was a remote property, had once been a tied labourer's cottage on the edge of an intake farm, now abandoned – an intake being a parcel of land that has been reclaimed from the moors above.

At least Kevin did not play about with the job, made one loud noise – a shattering of glass that offended the twilight – cut his hand as he climbed in. Bootsie removed the splinters from the edge of the frame before ordering Janet through it.

'Oh, Kevin – why did you have to choose the kitchen window? I've got a meal to cook. I'm going to be frozen rigid.'

'Christ! What an effing dump!' Janet said.

Bootsie performed the rare gesture of parting the tangle in front of her eyes and gave Janet the benefit of a one-to-one facial confrontation.

'Now look, young lady. I said just now that I want this to be a civilized operation. We don't like doing what we're doing. It's forced on us by the ramifications of a *laissez faire* economy. But since it has to be done, let's do it with the makings of refinement. I thought you were a young lady of some polish. That's one of the reasons you're here.'

'Arseholes!' Janet said.

'What an articulate infant you are, to be sure. Now, as you can see, this isn't the Ritz. You can have beans on toast, spaghetti on toast, fish fingers or a boiled egg.'

'How far is it to a chippy?'

'You've heard the menu. Make up your mind.'

'What brand's the spaghetti?'

Janet ate with surprising appetite, putting herself at the maximum distance from the other two at a dirty little table covered with threadbare oil-cloth. She had stopped talking, and her silence seemed infectious. The three munched until there was nothing left on their plates but smears.

'What happens next?' she asked then.

'We shall be in touch with your father. As soon as he's paid up, you will be returned to his loving care.'

Janet considered this coolly.

'As a matter of interest, how much are you asking for me?'

'We haven't decided yet.'

'He'll break your effing heads open next time he sees you. You'll never be able to set foot in Bagshawe Broome again.'

'Leave us to worry about that.'

'For a third of the takings, I'll make things easy for you.'

'Get her out of my sodding sight,' Kevin said.

'Come on, Janet. It's time I showed you our guest-room.'

'No deal?'

'No deal.'

'Then don't be surprised if you have problems.'

She opened her schoolbag and peered into it.

'God! Algebra! The Treaty of Utrecht! And the reproductive system of the frigging newt. What a night's entertainment! Is there anything to read in this place?'

Bootsie indicated a row of eight books on a shelf alongside the fireplace: a *Readers' Digest* Compendium of seasonal gardening tasks; a ready reckoner – in pounds, shillings and pence; a paperback *Emmerdale Farm*; a Family Medical Guide, published before the discovery of penicillin; and a pocket New Testament, with the facsimile signature of Field Marshall French – a 1914 trench issue. Janet Morrison chose the Medical Directory for her bedtime reading.

Bootsie took her upstairs to a room unfit for occupation by a young lady of refinement. It smelled of damp rot and senile illnesses and its stained ticking mattress was bare of sheets or blankets. A horse-blanket had been nailed over the window and Janet, carrying out a tour of inspection as soon as she was left alone, found that the panes had been sealed off with small-mesh chicken-wire, with staples driven in every inch all the way round. The only useful implement she had with her was a nail-file whose point snapped off before she got any purchase with it. The light was an unshaded, cobwebby forty-watt bulb and she lay on the bed and turned the pages from a line drawing of a bronchitis-kettle to the anatomy of a naked but very modestly equipped male.

Her father woke briefly, but did not recognize his surroundings. His weight had compressed his left arm and leg into a temporary paralysis. He groaned as he turned over on to his back and he was asleep again before he could take serious stock of himself.

Timothy John Fawcett's voice on the phone was no sleepier in the evening than at any other time, but he was able to quote, apparently without reference to notes, a list of some eight properties whose siting and vacancy might well have attracted Bootsie and Kev. One of them was Lower Edge Cottage, the last building to remain relatively intact up on Royds Intake.

Bootsie and Kev were fighting like famished terriers. Janet got up silently and put her ear to the panel of the bedroom door. They were quarrelling about her – or, at least, about what value they should put on her. Kevin, who clearly shared popular local delusions about the Morrison fortune, was in favour of a five-figure sum. Bootsie, who belonged to the small profits, quick returns school, thought they should settle for fifty quid in used notes.

'That,' Janet said to herself, 'is an effing insult.'

But even at that, she was far from confident that her father would lob up. He was more likely to look round for somebody to thump, thump the wrong one, and perhaps put her in real jeopardy.

Half an hour later, Bootsie and Kev themselves came upstairs, their row still on. Kevin was complaining about the lack of amenities of this hovel, and Bootsie was pointing out that it was he who had found it.

'And what's more,' she said, 'it's ideal. Abso-effing-lutely i-effing-deal.'

Janet studied a photograph of an Edwardian patient with a drooping moustache and sad eyes, lying stripped to a loin-cloth on a hospital bed. An arrow showed amateur diagnosticians how to find MacBurney's point, the tenderest spot in the abdomen when appendicitis has dug itself in.

Silence eventually prevailed in the next room, but was soon broken by the rhythmical creaking of a bedstead that did not sound as if it were likely to stand up to the demands about to be made of it. Janet listened with the critical sensitivity of a connoisseuse, but when the couple reached the stage of respiratory distress and abandoned murmuring, she got up and hammered on the partition wall.

'It's worse than Tuesday and Saturday nights at our bloody house,' she shouted, and when her banging resulted in a cessation of the transports, it gave her such satisfaction that she actually grinned.

'Stop that hammering, you bloody little bitch,' Bootsie called through the wall.

It was some time before the proceedings got under way again. They were subdued, and came quickly to a climax of which the connoisseuse apparently did not think much. She screwed up her face.

'I hope they're not three-or-four-times-a-bloody-nighters,' she said.

Thirteen

Detective-Superintendent Tom Grimshaw had in a steel cupboard a reserve of cyclostyled sheets that were a great comfort to him at times of fevered activity. They were his shopping-lists of systematic routines, to be followed in standard emergencies such as royal visits, Bradburn Rovers at home to Bradcaster United, sit-ins at the Technical College, the annual Hemp Valley Fur and Feather Show, visits by HM Inspector of Constabulary and terrorism – the latter still a mere phantom on Grimshaw's horizon.

But Grimshaw, like the Boy Scout he had once been, liked to think himself prepared. Once the appropriate sheet was on his clipboard, he was assured of something vital to a policeman of his hypersensitivity: he knew that he was doing the Right Things in the Right Order. He could not be got at for negligence or inactivity. Even such a ruthless critic as his conscience could not accuse him of culpable omissions.

Called from his slippered television corner – because a Missing Child was a contingency in which he insisted on putting himself at the command-post – he clipped the check-sheet to his millboard, picked up the telephone and held a ball-point poised to tick off Measures Taken as he took them.

Descriptions circulated to mobile patrols – neighbouring forces – hospitals – bus-stops – railway stations – transport cafes –

The list extended to the heart-cramping menace of *civilian searchers – dogs – frogmen –* and Grimshaw was human enough to enjoy an element of narcissism: Field Marshal Grimshaw coolly directing operations from his Advanced Tactical Headquarters, hampered only by a phalanx of assistant chief constables, the chief himself (who could be guaranteed to misunderstand any report put before him, however simple) a mildly hostile local press and the bull-dozing iconoclasts of the media.

Then there was Mosley. Was Mosley going to be an additional obstacle on this case, needing an Action Sheet on his own account? Grimshaw knew that Mosley was in or about Bagshawe Broome. By some new devious stroke, he had contrived to get Beamish with him. Mosley and Beamish cared nothing for what might be on other people's clip-boards. They never operated from clipboards themselves. Their stock in trade was a mish-mash of so-called intuition and the irregular army of undesirables who were their informants. But Mosley and Beamish were known to be in midstream of this spate of thefts from unoccupied premises: it might be days before they even heard of the abduction of Janet Morrison from the middle of their patch. Should Grimshaw leave them in blissful ignorance, thus protecting his own flank from disastrous interference? The answer, alas, was No! Because the next line on the Action Sheet read *Local CID*. The divisional inspector, in this case Mosley, was entitled to be kept scrupulously informed of all developments. It said so in Grimshaw's own roneoed typescript, from which there could be absolutely no deviation.

Authorization of overtime – Grimshaw dictated the relevant instruction to a clerk. The system was running sweetly. It was good for a system to be taken out of its steel cupboard from time to time and made to run sweetly. It lubricated the cogs of communication and command. Moreover, there was always spin-off. In the welter of stimulated activity, other outstanding cases would sometimes be liquidated. In the Findlay case last year, there was a fifty per cent supplement to normal night patrols, but for which a peripatetic gang of cat-stealers would not have been picked up. And Wilby Watson, a borough councillor, would not have been caught urinating in Woolworth's doorway in Bradburn High Street.

Issue arms to trained marksmen? –

Grimshaw hardly thought that the search for Janet Morrison had yet come to that pass.

Mosley and Beamish also had an Action Sheet, in their case written on the back of an old envelope. They were agreed that the Morrison child was not likely to be lodged anywhere in Bagshawe. The decaying labourer's cottage up Royds Intake was one of two possible refuges that Mosley had marked with a cross, but as he pointed out to Beamish, the Morrison-Bootsie-Kevin Road Show was likely to be laid up during the hours of sleep. To avoid duplicated journeys, it would be as well to work outwards from Bagshawe. So Mosley and Beamish also picked up a few items of spin-off. They noticed that late-night lights were visible in the rear of Veronique's Boutique. In a boarded-up slum awaiting demolition in Coalpit Street, were several dozen crates of apricot jam, in 7 lb tins, that must have been missed during the haul earlier in the evening. In what used to be the cellar of the old co-op emporium, they found old Sammy Warburton asleep. Mosley advised extreme stealth, lest they wake him.

'But I heard someone at the station say he's wanted for theft from a clothes-line,' Beamish said.

'Aye, and if we take him in, we shall be stuck with him and his bloody clothes-line half the night.'

Beamish drove them up into hills that forecast one of the emptiest stretches of the Pennines. Luminous eyes stared at them stupefied from the bracken-fringed verges. Baby rabbits, unaccustomed to human presence, did not flee from their approach. Their first stop was an isolated country residence asterisked on Mosley's envelope: Waterbrigg Hall.

'Owner's on the Costa del Sol,' Mosley said, casually omniscient. 'If those two haven't done this place over yet, it won't be long before it comes up on their list.'

The gates were well padlocked, but a light was on in an upstairs bathroom window: perhaps on a crime prevention officer's advice.

'We ought to have contacted the keyholder,' Beamish said.

'Well, neither of us thought of that, did we?'

And before Beamish knew that anything was happening, the front door was open, and Mosley was putting something back into his pocket.

'I won't tell you who taught me how to do that. He went down for nine months. It would have been two years if I hadn't told Quarter Sessions how helpful he'd been.'

They trod prudently at first, but there was no one in the place. The central heating system had been programmed to come on for an hour twice a day. Power cuts had put it an hour behind.

'I can't help feeling that Kevin and friend have missed a chance here,' Mosley said. 'It has to be Royds Intake, then.'

Mosley had known the late occupant of the derelict hovel: Harry Johnson, farm-labourer, widower for three-quarters of his adult life. He had been allowed to stay on in what had once been a tied cottage when the farmer himself had given up. Mosley found Kevin's tyre-marks in and out again. He found the broken kitchen window, was able to tell from the state of the cracked putty that it was freshly done. He found the evidence – unwashed up – of the meal that had been eaten here, counted three plates.

But the three people were not there. It was 2 a.m. – something over three hours since they would probably have gone to bed. He found the Medical Guide that Janet Morrison had been studying. He found her schoolbag and books. And there were doubtless many Holmes-like deductions that he could have based on the movements of furniture, the disturbance of dust, a dropped hair-grip, Bootsie's dustbin-liner of underwear and Kevin's Walkman cassette player. But there was nothing among this trail of trivia that told him where the trio had gone or why. There was still lukewarm water in the kettle, from which he hazarded the time of their supper: a neat calculation, but a futile one. There were no signs of any violence, other than the blood from Kevin's cut hand. There was nothing to suggest that anyone but the three principals had been here.

So why the sudden departure? It must have been unplanned for them to have left all their belongings – and especially for Kevin to have abandoned his source of music.

97

'Perhaps,' Beamish said, 'they saw our lights as we came up, and they've melted into the environment.'

'Their car isn't here,' Mosley said. 'If they'd left after they'd seen us, we should have seen them.'

Nevertheless they searched the yard, the coal-bunker, a collapsing henhouse. Nothing. If they had taken to rough country, they could be anywhere. Mosley pushed his homburg to the back of his head.

'This,' he said, 'is a bit of a bugger.'

Miles Morrison woke again, roused by the strain on his bladder, which although distended by years of abuse, was not of that infinite capacity facetiously claimed for it by some of his friends. He was still not conscious enough to connect his surroundings with recent events, but did at this time at least grasp the pattern of them. He recalled his prison sentence of years ago, and he believed that he was still serving it. Then he noticed that the cell door was open, a gesture made on Mosley's orders to show that he was not under arrest. But he did not see this, thought of it only as a token of the incompetence of the screws.

'The silly sods!'

He got up, went out into the corridor, found the lavatory and came back to his cell, this time shutting the self-locking door for himself.

The Topladys slept fitfully, and never both at the same time, in the five-foot double bed in which their entire family, five saints and a sinner, had been procreated. Involuntarily, as he tossed, Kitchener threw his arm about Primrose, drawing his chest close to her bosom. She was furious.

'Kitchener! How could you think of *that* at a time like *this*?'

Detective-Superintendent Grimshaw was still ticking off operational orders as he issued them.

Hospitals –

He had just set a detective-constable phoning round. There was confusion about an incident at the Hempshaw Cottage Hospital, whose casualty ward was trying to contact the police at the precise time that the police were trying to contact them. The detective-constable, bewildered by a complex story badly told, introduced complexities of his own as he reproduced for Grimshaw's benefit what he took to be the gist of it. And Grimshaw, leaping to an unjustified conclusion when the narrative was barely under way, listened with a sense of confusion quite worthy of his chief constable.

'They can't have.'

'They assure me they have, sir.'

'Sometimes patients discharge themselves, Hollins. But a midnight escape from a children's ward –'

'She was not in a children's ward, sir.'

'You said she was a child, Hollins.'

'Yes, sir. But she was not in any ward at all. As I understand it, she was on her way to a ward. With acute appendicitis, sir. And they lost her.'

'That hospital must be damned careless. Have they informed the next of kin yet?'

'No, sir. They don't know who she is.'

'Ring them again, and get a description, Hollins.'

'They've already given me one, sir.'

And it fitted Janet Morrison to the eyebrows over her shining forehead.

'I'll get over there at once,' Grimshaw said, issuing a plethora of orders that would have been carried out in his absence anyway.

'We'd better do a round of telephoning,' Mosley said. 'Bus stations, railway stations, lorrymen's pull-ups, hospitals –'

'Gone to the Costa del Sol for the winter,' Bootsie said. 'This will do us a treat. And it's damned sight better than the last place. The only thing is, there are certain rules. You'll have to put yourself in my hands – I'm a practised operator. Some things are obvious, like lights, and keeping away from windows. It's more than a series of precautions – it's a way of life.'

'I'm not a fool, you know.'

Bootsie parted enough of her hair to reveal one piercing eye in its entirety.

'No. I can see that. You're a crafty young bitch. And if I hadn't shot up those hospital stairs five at a time, I'd have lost you. The only difficulty is going to be my mobility. Kevin's pissed off with the wheels, and if I borrow from a car park, I may be seen driving up here.'

'Pinch yourself a bike,' Janet said.

'You unfeeling young devil. Do you know when I last pedalled up a hill?'

'It'll be worth it,' Janet said. 'My Dad's loaded. If he doesn't think I'm worth five grand, I'll bloody well leave home.'

Grimshaw parked in a space reserved for consultants, for which there was no competition at this hour. He got out and found himself alongside a blue Escort belonging to the same Force as himself. He could not tell to whom it was on charge. He found his way to the night sister in command of casualty.

'Well, you see, it was these two. They came in carrying a child, roughly wrapped up in a filthy blanket –'

'Steady,' Grimshaw said. 'Which two?'

'We don't know. The duty nurse hadn't time to ask them their names. She did what I'd have done – she put the patient first. The child was moaning and tossing. Nurse MacMichael put her hand down on her tummy, asked her where it hurt most, and when the child screamed, it left her in no doubt whatever. She had me bleeped, called for a porter, got the child on to a stretcher and into the lift, ready to go up at once to Ward Four. When she went back to the desk, the two who'd brought the girl had gone.'

'Describe them to me.'

'He looked like an escapee from a disco. She had so much hair hanging all round her, you couldn't tell whether she was coming or going.'

'And can you describe the girl?'

This was superfluous: she repeated what D-C Hollins had reported.

'So what happened to her?'

'That's what has us worried stiff. The porter was distracted because a casualty who'd sawn his thumb off had fainted. And when he turned round again, the lift had gone up. It seems to have stopped at an intermediate floor – the nurses' cafeteria, as a matter of fact. And the stretcher and the trolley were both empty. That's all there is to tell.'

'And do you really think that the child had appendicitis?'

'She gave that impression. She described all the usual symptoms. She got MacBurney's point exactly.'

'She can't have gone far, then?'

'I said she gave that impression, Superintendent. None of us examined her. No one had the time. All Nurse MacMichael did was an elementary palpation.'

'You are suggesting that she was putting it on?'

'I can't say whether she was or wasn't. We had less than two minutes in which to reach any conclusion at all.'

By the time Grimshaw reached the consultants' white lines again, the blue Escort had gone. Mosley did not believe in risking the formality of a nursing sister where as voluble a source as a night porter was available.

'It looks as if she's given them the slip,' Sergeant Beamish said. 'I suppose we'd better check whether she's gone home.'

'Do that, Sergeant Beamish. Then I think we might have a go at picking up Kevin Toplady.'

'And the girl. Don't you think she'll be with him?'

'Probably not for the next hour or two. He'll go back for his radio. Bound to. Can't live without it.'

'What does it feel like, having it in?' Janet asked.

'Don't you ever think of anything else, you disgusting little horror?' Bootsie said.

'Don't you ever *do* anything else?'

101

'You'll find out soon enough. How old are you?'

'I'm thirteen. And two girls in my class have found out already.'

'And what did they think of it?'

'They didn't like it much. They're both drips.'

'Maybe they are, maybe they're not. I used to think I knew who were the drips in this world. Nowadays I'm not so sure.'

'You must be going off a bit, to start talking like that.'

'O.K. then. You want to know what it's like the first time. You think he's coming at you with a bloody telegraph pole, that's what it's like. Then when you're just beginning to relate to it, you find he hasn't got a telegraph pole – only a fag-end of chewed-up garden hose. That's what it's like.'

'You've got it bad over Kevin, haven't you? He looks such a clot to me.'

'You'd better keep your opinions to yourself, young lady, if you don't want my hand to slip.'

'Well, you must think there's something more to him than his what-not. He finished too soon last night, didn't he? I heard through the wall.'

'What do you expect with you hammering and shouting? Many a man wouldn't have been able to do anything.'

'My mum and dad have been married twenty-three years and he still never lasts more than five minutes. I hear them every time they do it.'

'I wonder what you and your friends ever find to talk about?'

'He must be a clot,' Beamish said. 'Just look at the light that he's showing.'

An unshaded bulb was switched on behind an uncurtained upper window up Royds Intake. Beamish said afterwards that they ought to have been put on their guard by the fact that the radio was not playing. Except for the arhythmical orchestration of gutters, loose window-frames, leaking water and bits of hanging wire that were tapping and rattling, the house was in silence. Beamish and Mosley rushed up to the lighted bedroom, following the infantry theory that a hostile house is best searched from the top. They found no one there. All the things – Janet's school-bag, Bootsie's grubby underlinen and Kevin's Walkman had gone, and they had hardly had time to take this in when they heard a car start up, further up the hill, along the lane-end that merged with the moors – a section of road that no one else had used tonight. The vehicle went pelting down the hill without lights. Kevin must either have seen or heard them coming. It was a simple trick that he had played.

'Maybe he's not such a clot,' Mosley said.

Beamish went charging down the stairs, out of the front door and along the garden path.

'Waste of time,' Mosley told him. 'With the choice of roads he's got a mile lower down, we don't stand a chance. I hate to say this, Brother Beamish, but sooner or later we are going to be invited to give an account of ourselves to Brother Grimshaw.'

Fourteen

Miles Morrison was wakened, gingerly, by the least experi-
enced constable in the division, who had been sent down
with a mug of tea and a bacon sandwich and to tell him that
he was free to go after the desk-sergeant had had a word
with him. Morrison recoiled from the sandwich and began to
remember. A terrifying picture assembled itself. He rushed
up to the outer office.

'Will somebody tell me what's going on? Have you found
my Janet yet? And if you haven't, why are there three of you
hanging about in here?'

Sergeant Hammond was a diplomat *manqué*.

'I'm very sorry, Mr Morrison. We have not found your
daughter yet. Detective-Superintendent Grimshaw, the
most senior detective in the Force, has taken personal
charge. Every available man is deployed, men have been
called in from their days off, the Manchester boys are
working with us, as are the West Riding and the County
Boroughs. We have dogs out, an army battalion from
Preston and two helicopters from Air-Sea Rescue.'

Miles did not look convinced.

'Why is this happening to me of all people?' he asked.

'I think I can honestly say that we have had every available
resource applied to his case since eight-thirty yesterday
evening,' Grimshaw said. 'All except for two officers, who
ought to have been the most closely involved, and who could

not be found at the critical hour: two officers who appear to have forgotten that the gravest transgression in any police force in the world, from Wogga Wogga to Moscow Central, is to try to go it alone.'

He stopped, to see what their faces were saying. Beamish was standing at parade-ground attention. Even Mosley had the courtesy to be standing still. But nothing in his expression suggested that he had been listening.

'Have you anything to say, inspector?'

'Nothing,' Mosley said, as if that in itself was a statement of substance.

'Sergeant?'

'Only that I think you are being less than fair, sir.'

'I am being professional, Sergeant Beamish, which I seem to remember was one of the hallmarks of your work until I allowed you to fall into misleading company.'

'We had to come to a decision on the spur of the moment. We would have lost track, if we had come back to report.'

'And what have you done as matters stand, but lose track, Sergeant Beamish? You have caused us all to lose track.'

'Moreover, sir, I submit that it is hardly professional –'

'Moreover, Sergeant Beamish, I prefer not to be lectured on professionalism from the eminence of three stripes.'

Grimshaw was doing his best to maintain the momentum of his severity, but had an uncomfortable feeling that he was not doing very well at it.

'And moreover, for the remainder of today, the pair of you will work on one case until such time as you have completed it. you will carry out a teasel-thorough search of the Holgates' domestic premises. You will compare his possessions with every stolen property list for the last five years, and you will produce enough evidence to support a receiving charge.'

Beamish's poker face was now as unrevealing as Mosley's. Mosley even looked as if he were devoid of average intelligence.

'And Sergeant Beamish –'

'Sir –'

Beamish's eyes were focused on a spot on the wall well above Grimshaw's face level.

'Oh, get out of my sight,' Grimshaw said. 'There's a warrant, by the way, to turn the Holgates' place over.'

'There used to be,' Mosley said, when they were out of Grimshaw's office, and treading a safer corridor, 'a wartime expression much favoured by exuberant young men such as fighter pilots, rear gunners and the like. They used to say *Whack-oh!* when presented with any unexpected stroke of fortune. I say *Whack-oh!* Sergeant Beamish.'

'Indeed?'

Rebukes always disturbed Beamish, just or unjust.

'*Whack-oh!* Sergeant Beamish, we are now entitled to spend the whole day with the Holgates if we wish. But I take it we prefer to spend the day following our own inclinations?'

Miley was bewildered by what happened when he entered his house. His Emily was normally so submissive that he was in danger of hating her for it. For the first two minutes after his return to his hearth, she said nothing at all.

'I've just came back from the copper shop –'

He said it as if they had called him in for specialist consultation.

'Aye. The copper shop. Your only daughter stolen in the street, and your answer is to get drunk and incapable. If you ask me it isn't only money somebody wants, though we shall be having to find more of that than we've got. It's to teach you a lesson – for trying to be what you never were. For boring people stiff with your big-headed ideas. For bragging all over the place about what you've got in the bank.'

He crept out of the house again. The pubs were not yet open, otherwise he would have gone in for a hair of the dog and probably ended up paralytic again by midday. There was nothing for it but to repair to his magisterial spot on the Market Place – something that he felt strangely unwilling to do, for he did not need to be told how much face he had lost. He had been taken for a ride and had no solution. He knew that he could not call a posse of his cronies round him and issue them with short, sharp orders. He could think of no orders to issue.

He went to the Market Place nevertheless. His spot was still vacant. In his bleakest moments he had even pictured some bastard attempting a takeover: at least, that would have meant a thumping match he knew he could not lose.

His lieutenants were dotted about the square, looking oddly like mere loafers this morning. He took up his position. Some men took a step or two forward. Some braced their shoulders. Others followed suit. A man who was not entitled by protocol to sit on the horse-trough got up and retreated with sheepish discretion to the asylum of a shop doorway.

The life of Bagshawe Broome went on around them. The Pakistani dustman heaved a bin into the truck. The accountant of one of the High Street banks crossed the street and went into Veronique's Boutique. Miley glowered, waited. Then he had an idea. He beckoned Ben Eagle with a meaningful head-jerk and the two both went to the trough.

While Bootsie was out of the grounds, Janet removed all the dust-covers from the drawing-room furniture, which Bootsie had specifically forbidden her to do. She dumped the bulky cloths in a morning-room. The drawing-room was chintzy and needed a fire in the hearth. She sat in various armchairs, divans and chesterfields in turn, on the edges of them at first, but settling back eventually into vastnesses from which she could only get up again by swinging her legs violently.

She went over to one of the bookcases, examined *The Joy of Sex*, a paperback guide to relaxation and a prestige edition of the *Decameron* in a tooled leather binding. It was the latter that she took to read. But something was happening to the light reflected in the panel of the bookcase. She jumped guiltily backwards and saw that two cars had stopped for someone to open the gate and that the first of them was now entering the drive. She darted out of the room and flew up the main staircase. Enter Detective-Superintendent Grimshaw, accompanied by one detective-sergeant, two plain-clothes men dressed as if to infiltrate a ring of drug-pushers, one uniformed constable and the embarrassed and respectable keyholder.

'They're cracking on they're pulling all the stops out,' Miley said to Ben Eagle. 'Trying to make out they'd do as much for me as they would for Lord Muck. I'll believe that when it happens. And I'll tell you what: whatever they do to the bastard will be nothing to what will happen when I get my hands on him. If they give him ten years, I'll be waiting for him when he comes out.'

Then he saw that a figure was standing, patiently polite, some fifteen yards from him, waiting for the conversation to be over. Miley knew the man: Allen Durkin, one of Bagshawe's resident detective-sergeants.

'Could I have a word, Mr Morrison?'

Durkin had had words with him many times in the past, but this was the first time he had ever called him Mr.

'Detective-Superintendent Grimshaw wants to know if you've received any demand for money yet.'

'Not unless it's been delivered at home in the last half-hour.'

'The moment you do, let us see it at the station, please. Don't in any circumstances part with any money or come to any arrangements. Do you get that?'

Miley's natural reaction was not to get anything that issued from Sergeant Durkin's lips. But he remembered the figure of Janet waiting for her bus.

'I get it all right. When are you lot going to do something about it?'

It was only a few minutes' walk to the Holgates' home, but Mosley insisted on their being driven there. Beamish's inner spirit quailed at the magnitude of the task that Grimshaw had set them – and even more at Mosley's implication that they were not going to do it.

Avril Holgate looked like a woman not at all happy to see them, but making a brave show of concealing her feelings. Mosley asked to use her telephone and rang for a taxi to come for them here. Then he struck up an absurd bid at small talk about the effects of the first frosts on nasturtium vines.

'Mr Mosley – is there something –?'

108

But now their taxi was at the door and Mosley was on his feet saying goodbye. He had not mentioned the search warrant.

'You don't think it's necessary to carry out the detective-superintendent's instructions, then?' Beamish said.

'They've been carried out. Hasn't young Holgate been through his stock item by item? Who'd know better than he does where it all came from? I had to put enough pressure on him until he did it, and I'm buggered if I'm going about doing big jobs twice. Or little ones, either, for Tom Grimshaw's amusement. You and I have better things to do. I shall happen get it in the neck for using a squad car to come quarter of a mile, but at least that proved to Grimshaw that we're turning Dickie Holgate's dump over.'

Grimshaw did not see his way to sending a man to Ripon to lift a corner of the veil behind which Bootsie Bateman's parents had their being. The assignment fell to WPC Mary Carlyon, from the local station, to whom it appealed, because it was the first time for some weeks that she had done anything but exercise unglittering vigilance over the perils besetting bored market-town adolescents.

She went at breakfast time, formally observed in the dining-room. Bateman claimed that he could tell which of his clerks ate at their kitchen tables: you could smell the bacon fat in their clothes.

She chose breakfast time because she knew there would be tight timing in which she could create the maximum embarrassment and tactical advantage. She could also picture Bateman's office, the image of working pressures, his exhibitionist command of a hard-pressed team. They would be interrupted by telephone calls. There would be the shortest of intervals before his next appointment. A secretary would enter the room, look dismayed and go away again. His eye would keep wandering down to mail already opened for him.

He was a tax consultant: the world of difference had to be noted between tax avoidance and tax evasion. He was a man of reliable habits: at twenty past eight, halfway through his third cup of tea, he would be needing to go to the lavatory.

Mary Carlyon had said immediately that she had come about their daughter Elizabeth. Bateman had at once recited what was obviously his standard disclaimer: the young woman was of age. She had had everything made. No pressure had ever been put on her to do anything that she did not want to do. (He did not list those things that she might have wanted to do and that he had scathingly discouraged.)

'I'm afraid it is not given to a mere mortal like me to understand the workings of mind of a young lady who has had every opportunity, social, educational and personal.'

Mrs Bateman looked as if she was in fear of an eruption that might put her husband's vascomotor system at risk. She was wearing a long quilted housecoat in royal blue and pressed a cup of Earl Grey tea on the WPC.

'Having said that, she knows she has a home to come back to, a bedroom in which nothing has been disturbed since she left: her books, her gramophone records, even her dolls and school exercise books. She has only to give us one little assurance: that she will respect our standards.'

Which included, WPC Carlyon noted, the annual Conservative Association Ball, fake horse-brasses, wall-plates bearing reproductions of Dickensian inns and a brochure for a bridge-playing guest-house party on the North Wales Coast.

'Do you know her present whereabouts?' Mary Carlyon asked.

'We have not been accorded that privilege.'

'Or her associates?'

Edmund Bateman shuddered.

'When was she last home?'

The policewoman's Cornish accent lent, oddly enough, a sense of piquant realism to the conversation: she was so far outside the Batemans' orbit, and yet so closely involved in its detail.

'She has not really lived here since the end of her college career. That is to say at the end of her first and only year at that long-suffering establishment. We have been honoured by the occasional and fleeting visit, some of them lasting as

110

long as twenty minutes. By some curious coincidence, she has always been back when she has wanted something. Camping equipment it was once – something left over from her schooldays. Another time she came from a far corner of the country to collect a recording by a group called, I think, the Stones.'

'And to replenish her milk supplies?' Mary Carlyon murmured, with no hint of provocation.

'That was another thing. Her mother had a coffee morning in aid of Bangladesh, for which she had ordered three extra pints. Young madame departed without a hint of leave-taking, and the milk went too. All of it.'

Mr Bateman got up from the table and crumpled his napkin over his side plate.

'Has she been stealing milk elsewhere, then? Or are mere parents not entitled to know why their offspring are of interest to the police?'

'I don't really know any details, Mr Bateman. This is a routine enquiry. But if she does come home again in the near future -'

'We shall be happy to do all we can to help you to get her off our hands. And now, if you'll excuse me -'

Everything that happened in Bagshawe Broome was duly noticed by somebody. At least seven shopping housewives saw Primrose Toplady take a large tin of middle-cut salmon from a supermarket shelf and pay for it at the check-out. There was still a generation in Bagshawe who could remember the day when a tin of salmon was the standard, indeed the only permissible central offering on the upper working-class Sunday tea-table: soft spinal bones that melted between one's teeth as the juices and vinegar were being soaked up by the sprinkled pepper. But these had only been small tins. A large tin was unheard-of, save for a massive family visitation.

But since the war, eating habits had changed. In many a household high tea had been replaced by a later meal and tinned salmon had vanished as a regularity – a change in community ritual brought about mainly by price.

And here was Primrose Toplady buying a large tin in the middle of the week. Each of the seven housewives reported the event to an average of 1·5 others and it was not long before the Topladys' salmon was a talking point in their part of the town.

Janet Morrison could not understand why Waterbrigg Hall had two staircases, one central and imposing, one obscure and poky, and between the second and third floors, not even carpeted. When she saw Grimshaw and his storm-troops approaching the front door, her first instinct, like theirs, was to ascend rocket-like to the top of the building. And when they reached the third storey, by the main stairs, she went halfway down the servant's route. When they came down to the next floor, and one of them was detailed to investigate those backstairs, Janet was already back at the top and flattening herself into an alcove.

She could hear them talking loudly from room to room. They were not slow to conclude that intruders had been here. The keyholder was most concerned when he discovered how unceremoniously the dust-sheets had been treated. Grimshaw pounced on evidence of occupation: one of Bootsie's fresh cigarette-ends, the bed in which Janet had slept, still unmade. The consensus of opinion was that two of the fugitives had overnighted here, that they had gone off elsewhere and that they would be too cunning to return.

Janet heard them start their cars. She unflurriedly sat down with the *Decameron*.

Miley stuck his thumbs into his buckle-belt and surveyed the Market Place. His statement of vengeful intent had gone some way towards reasserting his position, but he knew that to make sure of it, he needed to master a memorable event. But then there was a freezing of eyes all round him. A spare but resolute figure was crossing the Square in a deliberate line towards him: Emily Morrison. She had never before been known to come here except to buy from stalls. And even then, she was careful to ignore her husband.

He looked at her neutrally, perhaps even prepared in certain circumstances to forgive her her trespasses. She handed him a sealed note.

'This was fixed to the clothes-line with a peg,' she said.

Miley tore the note open, read it and spoke to the world in general rather than his wife.

'I'm taking this to Mr Grimshaw. We'll see if he acts as big as he can talk.'

Mosley and Beamish were in sight of Waterbrigg Hall when they saw Grimshaw's convoy leave the front gate.

'Sit back in your seat,' Mosely said, and Grimshaw thus missed seeing who was in the taxi. But he was properly inquisitive about anyone approaching the Hall. He called his driver to stop, ordered his smaller car, by radio, to reverse and intercept the cab.

'Oh, it's Mr Mosley,' the messenger said. 'Mr Grimshaw's compliments, and would you be so kind as to come over and have a word with him?'

Beamish set his features. This was one to be played as it came; to be left, in the first instance, with crossed fingers to Mosley's inventive genius.

'And may I ask, Inspector Mosley, what brings you here at a time when I could have sworn I had assigned you a task elsewhere?'

'Indeed we are well on with that,' Mosley said.

'And are ready, no doubt, with an explanation of your less than desirable presence here?'

'Matching candlesticks,' Mosley said curtly. 'One of a pair at Holgate's. We've come looking for the other.'

And to Grimshaw's – and Beamish's – surprise, Mosley produced a candlestick from his overcoat pocket.

'And what makes you think you're likely to find it here?'

'Seems pretty obvious to me,' Mosley said.

'You know something that I don't, do you?'

'I would never suggest anything as bold as that, Mr Grimshaw.'

'No? And how, may I ask, had you hoped to gain entrance to the Hall?'

'I worked it out from first principles that this would be one of the first calls you'd be likely to make this morning. I'd been relying on you to let us in.'

'Had you now? But we'd already come out, hadn't we? Mosley – the assistant chief constable and I have made it plain on numerous occasions what the official policy is towards gaining unlawful admittance.'

'Blind spot in my mind,' Mosley said. 'I was overlooking the fact that you'd have locked up behind you. I suppose I would have had to send Sergeant Beamish haring after you for the key.'

'You and I, Mr Mosley, will go back together and look for that candlestick.'

'Aye,' said Hair-in-Rollers over her garden fence to Maroon Slacks. 'Full-sized tin, middle-cut. Must be expecting company.'

'Oh, she's got company. Arrived in the middle of the night. Headlamps on, doors slamming, shouting goodnight to the taxi-driver. Their Charles, I reckon, the one that's nearly a professor. He's the one she always sends for when they've trouble – especially when it's trouble over their Kevin. Then not above an hour ago the girl arrived, the one they crack on is musical.'

'I don't know where they put them all, in that house. If you ask me, it can't be decent.'

'Why's the back bedroom locked, mother?' Charles Toplady asked.

'I've got so much stuff stored away in there these days and what with all the crime there is about – Do you know there's four houses in this road been broken into in the last twelve months?'

'There never was a key to it in my time,' Grace said. 'I'd have given anything to have been able to lock myself in.'

'I got your father to fix it.'

'You got dad to fix it? You mean he actually got round to a job? Started on it, and finished it?'

'Now that's no way to talk about your father.'

'Well, how did he fix it? It's not a new lock. The old one's not been moved. From the state of the paint, I'd have said it's never been touched. How did he set about making a new key?'

'I don't know how he did it.'

She began to be as bad-tempered as she had been once when Charles had asked her a sex question at the age of eight.

'He's very clever with his hands, is your father. You children always did underestimate him.'

Grace sniffed noisily. Her eyes were fixed on a new photograph of her parents on a coach outing to Bolton Abbey. The Toplady children always reacted with subconscious unease if they came home to find anything different in the house.

'If you wouldn't mind moving up to the corner, Grace, I'll lay the table for your father. He's always home on the dot of five-and-twenty past twelve, and I like to have his plate on the table by the time he's washed his hands.'

Kitchener opened the door punctually, went up to the bathroom the moment he had hung up his coat.

'What's come over the back bedroom?' he asked, as he tested shepherd's pie with his fork.

'I've locked it,' she said. 'There's been a man I don't like the look of hanging about the street every morning this week.'

'You've locked it? It won't lock.'

Neither Grimshaw nor Mosley saw any reason to worry about noise when they entered Waterbrigg Hall less than five minutes after Grimshaw's last visit. Janet Morrison therefore had plenty of warning time in which to skip up to the highest flight of back stairs.

In the vegetable garden behind the house, Bootsie had emerged from cover when she heard Grimshaw's team drive off. Now she again retreated behind last year's bean-sticks.

The only candlesticks that Mosley and Grimshaw could find were in unparted pairs.

Fifteen

Janet and Bootsie cut each other's hair. Exploring drawers and dressing-tables, Janet had found a roll-up holdall containing scissors, combs and clippers.

When Grimshaw and his satellites were clear of the neighbourhood, Bootsie came in from the back garden, full of adventure and only partially exaggerating her exhaustion. She had had a long walk to reach a main road, had failed in her attempts to hitch-hike through fear of raising her thumb. She had felt hunted in her life before, but this was the first time she had heard her own description on the morning radio, as a person the police wanted to talk to. Moreover, for the first time in her life she felt something else — something not at all unlike a cloud of guilt. And it seemed to her that every driver must be on the look-out for her.

Then she came to a transport cafe where a 1,000 cc Yamaha was parked. She went in for a sludgy coffee and a sausage roll and went through the rituals with the rider, Len Saunders, a bull-chested man of her own age who told her early on that he had not yet had sex that day. Unambivalently she let him understand that he would not have long to wait if he would carry out a few simple commissions for her. Her terms were strictly payment on completion but he refused to leave her at the cafe to wait for him.

So she had to ride to the outskirts of Bagshawe Broome on his pillion, the exhaust proclaiming his macho qualities as if the overpowered machine were an extension of his reproductive system. She did not dare show herself on the

116

pavements of Bagshawe, so got him to stop in a village where, with his co-operation as diverter of attention, she filled the poacher's pockets of her patchwork coat with eggs, beans, spaghetti, cheese and meat-loaf.

This was necessitated by the parlous state of her finances. Last night, after she had caught Janet at the cottage hospital, there had been nothing for it but to go to a telephone kiosk up the road and ring for an all-night taxi. She told the driver that she had taken Janet into casualty with a foreign body in her ear — all of this taking place in the ten minutes' grace before the hue and cry became effective. She had then had them driven, not to Waterbrigg Hall, but to an address some five minutes' walk from it. The fare had left her without the price of another convenience meal in her purse.

Now, having restocked, she sent her escort into Bagshawe, telling him how to get into the Morrisons' yard-garden, and giving him the note to peg to the clothes-line. Then he drove her to a deserted barn, known commonly as Redfern's, for the pay-off.

'Was it good?' Janet asked.

'Was it hell! To tell you the truth, I hardly knew it was happening. There are times when you have to close your mind to it. You'll learn.''

Her knight errant started to be sarcastic when she declined his offer to shack up with her for a week or two's permanency. She only got away from him by thumbing a lift in a Granada that stopped with screaming tyres — it was less than fifty yards from her when she signalled. The driver, *a lecherous old sod in his fifties,* looked sideways at her with an interest that she thought had something in it besides lechery.

'Did you let him do it too?'

'I did not. I wouldn't have. If it had come to the push, I could have run faster than he could. But I didn't think he was going to stop when I asked him to. I had to whip out his ignition key. That's the ploy, by the way, that's worth practising. Once the key's in your hand, you can always threaten to throw it over a wall, or into a pond or something. You can even actually throw it. So — here I am.'

She took her ungainly boots off, threw her socks across the room and eased her anything but clean toes.

117

'Do you know, I think I'll have myself a bath before I'm much older. I'll have a look at the central heating and get some hot water going. And I want you to cut this bloody hair off, before I'm picked up on the weight of it alone. Without it, nobody would know me: it's bloody years since anybody saw my face. Do you know anything about cutting hair?'

'Shouldn't think there's much in it, is there? I trimmed one of my dolls once, when I was a kid. Caused a hell of an effing stink at home. I'll tell you what: I'll have a go at yours if you'll do mine.'

'What do you want yours done for? You've got nice hair.'

'Who the hell wants to be bloody nice? It makes me look about six. Do you know how long it takes to do every morning?'

'Please yourself. It's all the same to me.'

'We could post these damned pigtails home, if they don't come over with the cash the first time of asking.'

'That's a thought. Even if it has been done before, it must be a bit of a shock, when they open the parcel. If it doesn't work, we could always follow up with one of your ears.'

'Sod off! You know what you can do to yourself.'

'It's some time since I was reduced to that strait.'

They did their hair-dressing in one of the bathrooms. Janet began by parting Bootsie's curtain, then hacking it down to something that she could tentatively sculpt. Bootsie shook her head and shoulders when they were free of the tangle.

'My God – why've I been carrying that load around with me?'

'Is that what your Hell's Angel said this morning?'

'Don't be so bloody revolting, Janet. Honestly – don't be so revolting. Do you think we could live together for a few hours without talking like a pair of dirty-minded toddlers?'

Janet went silent, stood back and assessed the shape of what was left on Bootsie's head. She then began clipping here and there, stopping frequently to see what sort of a balance was evolving.

More clipping. Janet clammed up.

'I hope you're not going to sulk, just because I made a civilized request,' Bootsie said. 'If you want to look grown-

up, you've got to show a bit more maturity than you have up
to now. There's nothing wrong with sex. Sex is *there*. With
the right fellow, in the right place at the right time, sex can
be fine, bloody fine. But it's hardly news. But don't you
worry, kid. I was like you once.'

'I wish you wouldn't keep calling me a kid.'

'Sorry. You're more grown-up for your age than some I've
come across.'

Bootsie examined the interim handiwork in a mirror.

'Funny. I only let it get this way out of pig-headedness.
The reason I left home, my hair was. Well – I'm not saying
there weren't a few other things. But my hair was the last
straw. Always being told to get it out of my eyes. Christ! I
had hardly any in those days. Then I didn't keep an
appointment they'd made for me to have it done – then
came the shoot-out. I told myself I'd never have a pair of
scissors near me for the rest of my days. And I've stuck to
that till now. How bloody stupid can you get? OK. Clip on.'

'You need a neck-shave.'

'I expect her ladyship has a twee little razor she digs out
her armpits with.'

They found one, and Bootsie started laughing.

'I'm a smart bloody kidnapper, aren't I – letting my
victim loose on me with a razor.'

'I'm not your victim. We're in this together.'

'We are now. For pretty much the same reason, I should
imagine. You're pretty fed up with your folk too, aren't
you? They're rolling in money, I suppose?'

'My dad's a tinpot crook. And he pisses the living-room
fire out every night before he goes to bed.'

'Charming. What's his line, then? Land development?
Stock market? Or cat burglary?'

'Street-corner monkey business.'

'My old man's dead respectable. Works out ways the well-
off can claim for capital expenditure they've never
expended. And always on about what the youth of today is
coming to.'

'My dad's been to prison.'

'Mine only ought to have.'

'For grievous bodily harm.'

'Thanks for warning me. I'll try to keep my distance. What's he going to do to you when he gets you back?'

'Buy me some sort of present, I hope. He's never going to know I was in on this. He thinks I'm purity and innocence.'

'How do you want your hair?'

'Close to my scalp, but not skinhead.'

'It's a pity in some ways,' Bootsie said. 'You have marvellous hair.'

'That's what they all say. That's why I want rid of it.'

First one, then the other pigtail fell to the floor.

'You know,' Janet said. 'I wouldn't have said that Kevin was your type.'

'That's something you wouldn't understand. No, sorry – I'll unsay that. I believe you might understand. A girl meets somebody, and that's it. It has nothing to do with similar tastes or background – or even your honest opinion of the man – if you've got one. It's something to do with chemistry – bio-chemistry. Vibes. There are such things. We spend half the time fighting like two cats with their tails tied together over a clothes-line. We've split up a dozen times – and couldn't stand it. Neither of us could sleep or eat till we got together again. You're from Bagshawe Broome. You must know the Topladys.'

'I've seen them about. They don't have anything to do with us. Clever lot, aren't they?'

'Think they are. Only Kevin isn't like the rest of them, as I think you've seen for yourself already. But the image he had to fit in with was there before he was shagged for.'

'Now who's talking rough?'

Bootsie held a hand-mirror to the side of Janet's head.

'Do you want it any closer than this?'

'That'll do fine.'

'You have a mother, too, I suppose.'

'Pitiful. Trodden on and lets it happen. Has about three ideas in her head and comes out with them every ten minutes.'

'You're lucky. Mine hasn't got three – but that doesn't stop the flow. What are you going to do with your share of these earnings?'

'Savings bank. I'm leaving home as soon as I can get away

120

with it, and I don't mean to rely for my bread on parked Yamahas.'

There was no more that Bootsie dared do to Janet's hair. She walked all round the child. She had not done a bad job, and it was what the kid wanted. But the teenage cranium was too small to stand up to the close-sculpted effect. Her high forehead looked somehow absurd without a fringe. Janet's eyes were sharp and sardonic, but there was a lot that was beyond their experience.

When Miles Morrison went to the police station with the ransom note, he was ready with a wealth of scathing wit about the inactivity of the fuzz, but things worked out differently. He was seen immediately by a young detective-sergeant, a stranger on *ad hoc* secondment to Bagshawe Broome, with a hint of college training behind his fluency and a range of vowels that neither Lancashire nor Yorkshire would have owned. Even Miley had to concede that he knew what he was talking about. Miley did not even have to announce who he was. He did not have to remind Sergeant Harman of any detail. The sergeant knew the case and the people inside out.

'The old quarry-face in Penscar Wood. I dare say you know the place?'

'Can a duck swim?' Miley answered brightly.

'You're to go there between eight and nine tomorrow night, taking five hundred pounds in used notes – '

Bootsie had reduced the demand without consulting Janet. She believed she was being realistic.

'We have prepared a package for you – '

This work of art was the triumph of one of the Bradburn backroomers. On the top and bottom of each wad there were real notes. Glued together in the middle there were false ones, with convincing edges. The packet would not stand up to close examination – but in Penscar Wood there would be not time for counting.

'You will deposit your parcel under a stone that will have been marked with a lick of yellow paint. Your daughter will be waiting for you at the Comstock Fiveways crossroads as soon as the payment has been collected. Mr Morrison, you do understand, don't you, that things are now in our hands? Do not try to take any initiative, or something could go catastrophically wrong. You'll be under our discreet – I hope, indeed, invisible – surveillance both in the Wood and at Fiveways.'

Miley was none too happy about this.

'There was that bit in their note where they say what they'll do to our Janet if I don't come along – '

'Ignore that. They'll do nothing.'

'Won't they be desperate?'

'They're not the sort of people we're greatly worried about, Mr Morrison.'

A ripple of adrenalin enlivened Miley's veins.

'Is it true that one of them is that young Toplady? If I get my hands on him –'

'And do you think he doesn't know that? This is not an intelligent crime, Mr Morrison. We do not expect difficulty. Our main concern will be to avoid accidents. And I know what you must be thinking. I'm sure I would feel the same in your position. But it will be over when you get your daughter back.'

'If they've marked her in any way – if they've upset her, Mr Harman – '

'You mean you saw the Bateman girl in the grounds while you and Grimshaw were in Waterbrigg Hall?' Sergeant Beamish said.

Mosley nodded unexcitedly.

'I spotted this movement in the vegetable garden, you see, and kept myself within spitting distance of the back windows.'

'And you didn't tell Grimshaw? We had enough men on the grounds to have picked her up there and then.'

'And what would we have gained by that?' Mosley asked, in a tone that had Beamish doubting his own intelligence.

'We'd have arrested a kidnapper.'

'There are two kidnappers, Sergeant Beamish, one of whom we can trust to look after the child, if only in her own interests. In a corner, the other might do anything. At the moment, those two are apart. Presently, they'll get together again, as they always do. That'll be the time to strike.'

'But wherever she is, you're leaving the child at risk.'

'She's survived living with her father. If you were trying to earn your keep in the Bateman-Toplady fashion, you'd watch how you treated Miley Morrison's daughter, wouldn't you?'

'Buying this big tin of salmon this morning,' Mrs Selby said. 'Then in the afternoon she's round at the building society. Do you reckon they've come into money? I've heard of nobody dying – and we would have, wouldn't we, Mrs Hinchcliffe?'

'Do you reckon she must have been drawing some out, then?'

'I'll find out, Mrs Hinchcliffe. I'll find out.'

While his mother was out withdrawing her savings, and his sister had gone out to visit some girl she had been at school with, Charles Toplady could have sworn he heard music coming somewhere in the house: not the sort of music that the Topladys patronized – a faster-than-pulse beat with the bass drum dominating a core of amplified guitars, and with a lyric that was a single short phrase, repetitiously shouted rather than sung.

He started to climb the stairs, stopped to listen again. Now there was nothing to hear. He went up to the landing and put his ear to the panel of the suspect back bedroom door. He heard something in there: a light book, falling from the bed to the floor, perhaps the back of a hand catching against the bed-post. He thumped with the side of his fist.

'Kevin – are you in there?'

There was now the emptiest of silence. In all truth, the door was no daunting obstacle. The panels were of three-ply, as flimsy as one might expect from mass-building in the early thirties. He did not believe that the lock had been repaired. He did not believe that it was repairable. The door must be held by a bolt inside, probably of the kind that could be bought at any ironmongers and fixed with half a dozen half-inch screws.

'Kevin – I'm breaking in.'

He judge what run-up he could take. But his mother and Grace came back into the house at that moment.

'Charles – what are you doing up there? Come down those stairs at once.'

It was the voice of a woman who discounted her husband, who had rod-ruled five sons and a daughter, and had sent all bar one of them catapulting to success in a world that she barely understood.

'Charles, come down. I want to talk to you. In this family, when one is in trouble, he knows that the rest of us are standing by.'

Mosley announced, without giving Beamish time to compose himself for the strain, that they were going to the launderette. All this staying away from home wrought havoc with a man's intimate apparel. It was essential for Beamish to accompany him, because he always got muddled up over all this damned powder and stuff.

'I don't know how you come to think I'm an expert on detergents,' Beamish said.

'I always look upon you as a contemporary man, well up in microchips and what-not.'

'I hardly think any laundromat in Bagshawe Broome will turn out to be the last word in high tech, Mr Mosley. I heard a woman in the street saying that one of the machines broke down last week because it was clogged with dead fleas.'

'Any contraption that can disinfest the community on that scale is performing a vital public service.'

In working fact, there was an attendant who rose magnificently to the challenge of seeing that the old man knew which buttons to press and handed him a smeared paper cup two thirds full of a dirty-looking grey substance. And there was by now not a woman in the establishment who was not ready to leap to the inspector's rescue in case of overloading, stoppage or flood. Pretty soon Mosley's pipe was bubbling like a hookah as he sat, darkly amorphous in hat and overcoat, apparently fascinated by the vortices performed by his disreputable woollen undergarments as they tumbled about behind a glass panel.

Alongside him, Beamish was doing his best to look as if he and Mosley were strangers to each other, thrown together casually in the hurly-burly of modern aids to living. It was Mosley's woollens from which he most wished to dis-associate himself: yellow long-johns, with buttons of various styles and histories; a vest so hairy that one could have done penance in it; a pair of socks, darned diligently and often with whatever shade of yarn had been on hand at the moment. Beamish was not quite tempted to stand on his chair and broadcast his non-involvement, but he would have liked to assure the unknown woman on his left that nothing on display belonged to him.

Mosley seemed to be transported into some illusion of Nirvana. Before long his presence was no longer an event in the launderette and the conversation had picked up to its usual level.

'It turned out I was right, Mrs Hinchcliffe. It *was* money she was drawing out. Harriet Armstrong was there, and she told me – a great wad of notes, enough for many a crate of tinned salmon.'

'Well, I never did, Mrs Selby.'

'And she was not the only one. Do you know who else was in there, Mrs Hinchcliffe?'

'Search me, Mrs Selby.'

'Mrs Morrison, that good-for-nothing Miley's wife. Mrs Armstrong told me she drew out even more than Primrose Toplady.'

Sixteen

'I still don't see it,' Janet said. 'I wouldn't give him five more minutes of my time, and I wouldn't have needed five minutes in the first place to know what he is.'

'That's the difference between you and me,' Bootsie said. 'You're –'

'Don't start that again.'

A rapport had grown up between the two, promising, almost amounting to, a brittle friendship. But they had begun to get on each other's nerves.

'He's not nearly good enough for you,' Janet said.

'Haven't I already told you that that doesn't enter into it? Well: not much. He needs my help, and I need his.'

'I can believe the first part. But you only mean you're sorry for him.'

'I don't deny I am. It's all part of it. But it isn't everything.'

'From what you've told me about him, he can't help himself.'

'Ever heard of a late developer?'

'So when's he going to develop?' Janet made a derisive noise in the back of her nose. 'At least, I'm not going to earn my living thieving.'

'Bully for you. You've said that before. And I'll admit I sometimes feel a bit fed up with this way of life. I wonder how much longer I can stand it. I got a kick out of it at first. I suppose I thought I was getting at my father and his friends, who are nothing but large-scale, pompous and self-righteous bloody racketeers. I don't mean to go on for ever like this. I don't know what I shall do.'

'Have a family,' Janet said, not without mischief.

Bootsie shuddered.

'That's if you don't get caught tomorrow night.'

'That's the key question. I know the risk. Yes or no. Touch or go. Fifty-fifty. Bagshawe Broome roulette. I'm banking on your father not putting his trust in the police.'

'He won't.'

'And then he picks up that yellow-painted stone and finds your pig-tails and my note, he won't hang about long in Penscar Wood.'

'And I'm telling you it's your duty as a member of this family to do what I'm asking, Charles, and that's to get him away from Bagshawe Broome until the fuss has died down. Get him away from this town before something terrible happens to the girl. Then he can't be held to blame.'

'It seems to me that everything that matters has already happened, mother. The girl's been abducted.'

'But we haven't heard that she's come to any harm so far. If something goes wrong now, we can all swear we knew where Kevin was. I've got money for you to find him somewhere to stay.'

Primrose Toplady, on the downward grade of middle age, was looking jowly and mean-eyed – positively ugly in her effort to persuade her son. Charles was not her eldest. She knew better than to have sent for Eric. There were disconcerting signs that Eric was developing a mind of his own, but she still believed she could rely on Charles. Yet she knew intuitively that she was coming to the end of her ability to reason with him, and that she had so far failed. There was nothing left now but a sententious appeal to what a boy owed his mother. If that failed too, then the whole of her life's efforts were in ruins.

Charles Toplady, for two years now a sought-after tutor of final-year students, recipient only last week of a hint that the Holderness Fellowship was his for the application, sat avoiding his mother's eyes, and it was still not certain whether he was weak enough to do her bidding.

Kitchener Toplady, who had been the last of them all to learn that Kevin was in the house, sat in inarticulate misery. The dispute was beyond him. He knew that his wife's scheme was absurd and dangerous, but he did not know how he could influence her. Grace sat in one of the fireside chairs, picking automatically with a crochet hook.

'Mother – I'll not do it.'

The decision was made. The words were out. His mother looked at him, haughtily hurt and disdainful.

'He's not worth it, mother.'

'You're all worth the same to me,' she said.

'Is that why you won't have his picture on the wall?'

But saying that was a mistake. It was too cruel – and too true.

'What goes on my wall and what stays off it are my business, young man.'

'I'll not argue with that.'

'Let me tell you this –'

She was out of her corner for the second round.

'When I let your brother in, in the middle of last night, we had a very long talk.'

She spared a second for a derisive glance at Kitchener.

'*He* didn't even know I'd gone down to the door.'

How many very long talks had she had with Kevin in the past, Charles wondered. Had there ever been one that hadn't made current matters worse?

'Kevin has promised me –'

Had she never had promises from Kevin before? It wasn't worth saying anything.

'If you'd been there, Charles, you'd have seen how sorry he was.'

How scared –

'How he wishes he could do what you've all done.'

'He's had the same chances.'

She looked at Charles with a hatred he had never seen turned on him before.

'And how you've always preened yourself whenever he's been in trouble,' she said. 'You and his sister both.'

'Bring him down,' Charles said. 'Let him tell us for

128

himself how he thinks he's going to get out of this.'

Mrs Toplady looked at them in turn, as if she suspected new ridicule.

'I'll do that,' she said.

She went upstairs and they heard her knock on Kevin's door. Then she was halfway down again, calling for Charles with the shrillness of panic.

'He's not answering. Oh, Charles – you don't think – ?'

'Stand back, mother.'

Charles's shoulder did what he had contemplated this afternoon. The back bedroom window was open and a savage draught from the November night was blowing the curtains into the room. The bed was a crumpled mess. The room still bore evidence that it had once been his sister's: he had used her powder-bowl as an ashtray. But Kevin had gone.

Seventeen

It was Miley's habit to leave the Market Place half an hour before the shops closed. At that hour people were flocking out of works gates, where there were instalments to be collected and reminders to be issued.

The Market Place bore a different look at this hour. Miley's staff officers had gone home for their tea and the horse-trough was surrounded by juveniles on BMX bicycles who would later have to yield the place to their older brothers, angling for girls with the bait of their powerful Japanese machines.

On the day the ransom was to be paid, there was an additional change in the configuration of the square. Someone else had at last taken over Miley's square yard of strategic superiority. It was Mosley, standing some five yards south-south-east of Bert Hardcastle's sandwich stall, his heels nine inches apart, his feet at an angle of thirty degrees and his fingers lightly intertwined behind his back – a stance ingrained in him by the drill instructors of World War II. But in all other respects Mosley's bearing was unmilitary – as indeed it had been in World War II. He wore his hat with a stolid lack of panache. His shoulders were rounded. His chest was submerged in the shapelessness of his greatcoat and his abdominal muscles were relaxed to the point of sagging.

He had only one minion attendant on him, and he was not in sight. Sergeant Beamish was in the shadows in an alley leading to the rear areas of shops, from where he would keep an eye not only on Mosley, but also on Veronique's Boutique, which he saw another man approaching. This was Mr T. Howard Pendelbury, the heavily moustached and wearisome pompous clerk to the Bagshawe Broome justices. 'Veronique,' otherwise known as Bessie Bullough, fifty-five and looking it, let him in. The odd thing was that Bessie's absurdly large staff of ravishing young ladies – Beamish had counted eight of them – had already gone home. Was a night shift awaited?

Three women whose looks and figures would not have qualified them for Veronique's payroll, came into the Square and ambled the length of it three times, taking in the identity of the few bystanders, then changing direction with the confident intent of a skein of geese and homing in on Mosley. The ensuing conversation might have looked casual to some.

'We are not given to minding other people's affairs, Mr Mosley. Howsoever –'

'And begging your pardon if we are wasting your time –'

'Not that we make a habit of spying on our neighbours' visitors –'

It all led up to a denunciation of Kevin Toplady's escape down a drainpipe and across a series of twilit gardens, heading obviously towards the short length of uncompleted by-pass that would take him out of the town without his having to pass through it.

Mosley looked at them mournfully and did not even nod. Some thirty yards after they had left him, one of them looked back and saw that he had not moved a limb.

Bootsie's state of nerves surprised Janet.

'I hope you're right about your father. If he's in cahoots with the police –'

'He won't be. If I know nothing else about him, I know that. He wouldn't work with coppers if somebody had threatened to murder him.'

It had been a long day. They had sensed each other's tension, and had avoided friction by occupying themselves in different parts of the Hall. Janet had combed every bookshelf in every room and helped herself to an armful of erotica, every volume of which she found as unsatisfying as she had found the *Decameron*, which to her mind was childishly inexplicit. Bootsie spent the day in an upstairs room with a view of green hills ribbed by dry-stone walls, motionless in meditation that might have been transcendental. Neither of them wanted more than a nominal bite to eat.

Late in the afternoon Bootsie came looking for Janet, thinking she had better run through the changes she had made in their operational plans. In case Miley had proved untrue to form, the police would have taken steps that had to be foiled. She was going to leave a note under the yellow-painted stone fixing a different rendezvous for Janet to be picked up, and Janet had to go there by a carefully devious route that Bootsie had made her memorize.

'Janet?'

Bootsie had got used to shouting up and down the big empty house; it had seemed dangerous at first – and unmannerly.

'Janet – where the hell have you got to?'

But the question was not answered. Janet was nowhere to be found.

Penscar Wood was a plantation of some twelve acres that had been conceived in late Victorian times by a countrified industrialist keen on improving the view from his rural barracks. It was Janet who had told Bootsie about it, and it was ideal for their purpose. The wood was something of a joke in Bagshawe, and Miley was one of those who had found the retreat variously useful as he grew up. As a schoolboy he had gone there with others to smoke cigarettes in safety and to poke with sticks at the abandoned contraceptives in the notorious glades and dells. A few years later he had himself contributed to this litter.

He entered now like a man afraid of the dark, distrustful of the army of trees, disorientated not to have bricks and mortar round him and unresilient surfaces under his feet. The last time Miley had been here had been a moonlit summer night, more than a quarter of a century ago, in the company of a switched-on young lady who had been even more eager than he was to reach the heart of the vegetation. There had been rabbits on the edge of the wood that night, but now he could not identify the animals whose sudden movements startled him among the fallen leaves. The creatures whose proximity he most hated to think about were plain-clothes policemen, and once he was startled to see a bogey watching him: but the phantom turned into a dead tree that had lost its bark and most of its limbs to a stroke of lightning. There was, in fact, a disconcerting absence of the law: he had not spotted a single representative, and that worried him too: what the hell was everybody playing at?

His sense of direction was deficient, and several times he unknowingly circled the rock-face to which he was supposed to go, ending up on its top edge and almost falling twenty feet.

It had never been worked as a commercial quarry, but merely to provide stone for local barn-building. Miley clasped the packet that Sergeant Harman had given him and switched on his torch to look for the stone under which he had been told to deposit it. He could not find it at first, but then he saw where a small rectangular cavity had been dug to the depth of about a foot. A stone that could conveniently have covered it was lying a few feet away. Miley picked it up, turned it over and saw a daub of paint that in daylight might well appear yellow.

It was clear that the hole had been interfered with. Miley was not at the peak of his mental powers. He could not work out what might have happened Had some passer-by turned the stone out of curiosity? But what passers-by were there in Penscar Wood in the dark at this time of the year? Had it been someone who knew about the stunt that was going to be played, and had come early to lift the loot?

An owl flew silently over the quarry-space. Miley did not like owls. He did not like anything that impugned the security of civilization as he understood it: the unmenacing drabness of Bagshawe. Undergrowth stirred for no discernible reason: there must be someone behind there, another plain-clothes jack not ten yards behind him, another in front, obliquely to his left. But no, that was the stump of sycamore, its season's new growth waving like tentacles. Then loose stones slipped somewhere away to the right. Miley knew that he was not alone in the wood.

Field-Marshal Grimshaw sat on the front edge of the back seat in his staff car and made a finicky alteration to the chinagraph line on the talc over his map. There was all the difference in the world between his *Chevette* and the wartime Humber Snipe in which he pictured himself. He had read somewhere that Montgomery had been able to sleep in baby-like peace throughout a night in which his massed army-groups were going to launch a major assault. 'I need my rest,' he had said. 'The planning's done.'

That had never been Grimshaw's temperament. On the eve of battle he could not have brought himself to switch off the light, let alone close his eyes while there remained a chance that something might go wrong.

But like that other great commander, he had looked at, looked at again and better-looked at every detail in his plan. And as far as he could see, all those details had been as admirably executed as they have been thought out. A substantial task-force had been mobilized, briefed, deployed and had gone to ground in slit-trenches dug that morning to surround both Penscar Wood and the Fiveways Crossroads. The concealment of his troops was as perfect as could be. They had been told in six different ways – and had been made to repeat individually – that whatever happened in either place, no move was to be made against anyone until the safety of the child had been absolutely assured. Miley, Kevin, Bootsie, or any of the as yet unknowns who might be involved, were not to be accosted until Janet Morrison was in friendly hands.

Grimshaw was parked out of sight and without lights, in a lane off a B road. By daylight the spot overlooked the northwest corner of Penscar Wood. Thinking that Bootsie and Kev were the sort who might play about with CB radio, he had ordered wireless silence, so he was frustrated by almost total ignorance of what was going on over there. But he had been here since before the light began to fail and had seen Bootsie come along the B road, climb a gate and cross a field towards the trees. He had never met her, knew her only from her description, but even without her hair he had no doubt about who this was. She had to go into the wood early to paint her stone and prepare her cache. She did not return until the light was becoming all but impossible – and not improved by the binoculars through which Grimshaw was trying to survey the field. By the time she was back on the road, he was seeing her as dimly as Miley had seen spectral policemen at the quarry face.

She appeared to be about to walk west along the road when she was suddenly floodlit by the headlamp of a motor-cycle. The rider was a familiar type – huge, the jazzily painted helmet, the leather jacket, the roar of machismo exhaust. As he came abreast of Bootsie he slowed down with his clutch out and an orgasm of uninhibited throttle. He U-turned and pulled up beside her. Grimshaw assumed that this was Kevin, whom he had also never seen, but who he felt sure would own a motor-cycle. But if this were Kevin, he would have expected Bootsie to leap at once astride the pillion to be whisked away to where Janet was being held prisoner.

This did not happen. As far as Grimshaw could see, they were having an argument that went on for minutes rather than seconds, and the girl seemed to be keeping her distance from the bike.

Then she changed her mind. She mounted behind the rider, who turned again and rode off the way she had been walking. Grimshaw told his driver to start his engine.

'There are two things that could go badly wrong,' he said. 'We might lose them – or they might spot that we are after them.'

On the Market Place Mosley actually varied his stance. After the three women had gone away, he swung first one leg, then the other, brought his hand from behind his back and exercised his shoulders in a circular motion. Then he came away from the spot sanctified by Miley, to Bert

Hardcastle's kiosk. He bought himself a sandwich that must have contained a quarter of a pound of ham and walked up and down a ten-yard beat as he ate it. He took it for granted that Beamish was still keeping an eye on the boutique. He had seen nothing at all of the sergeant for the last half hour – had not even looked in his direction.

When he had finished eating, he moved over in casual fashion towards the boys with the bicycles, who were still congregated committee-wise about the horse-trough. He examined one of the more sophisticated-looking of their machines, and even asked if he might ride a few yards on it, which he did to universal delight with his knees splayed out and his coat flapping. But then they heard the heraldic arrival of the first mighty engine of the evening. The boys began to disperse. There was a clear-cut delineation of who was entitled to pride of place in the Market Place, and between what hours.

It was the most natural of sequences for Mosley to continue the same easy relationship with the young men when they began to gather. They knew him by reputation. It was common knowledge what he was involved in in Bagshawe Broome and it tickled their pride when he seemed to be taking a genuine interest in the lethally powerful machines which they straddled.

'What sort of bike does Kevin Toplady ride?' he asked.

There was the sort of laughter that proclaimed them a secret society.

'Kevin Toplady? Him?'

'He couldn't ride a kid's bloody tricycle.'

'Kev with a thousand cc between his knees? Mr Mosley, you'd have to get your lot to clear the roads.'

They clearly held Kevin Toplady in unqualified contempt – but Mosley did not give the impression of wanting to exploit this. He grinned and went on listening.

'That'll be the day, when Kevin takes off.'

'Bootsie'll have to hang on!'

'I saw Bootsie hanging on the other day,' one of them said.

'What – hanging on behind Kev?'

'No. Behind Len Saunders.'

'That randy sod! Where was this, then?'

'Up at Steve's, on the Waterbrigg road.'

'What – he picked her up there?'

'No. She picked him up. I heard Steve telling someone. She went off on the back of his bike. Then later on he was parked outside that old barn of Redfern's.'

'Well, there's more than one of us has had reason to be grateful for Redfern's. But she was taking a chance, wasn't she, using Steve's? Isn't that hers and Kev's usual hang-out?'

'In the evenings. This was in the middle of the morning. I don't know where Kev was.'

'Perhaps they've broken up again.'

Mosley saw – without appearing to take notice – that Beamish had come out of his alley and advanced into the open Square, ready to catch the old man's attention when it suited him.

'Well, when they've broken up before, it's generally in Steve's that they've come together again.'

Mosley moved over towards Beamish. Beamish was in a mood of pristine eagerness.

'I can see a feasible way round the back. I can easily get round there – and a cover story's no trouble.'

'Leave it,' Mosley said, almost curtly. 'There's a bigger and better fish than Bessie Bullough hiding in the reeds.'

'You hate everything,' his mother had said.

That had been the principal message of last night's very long talk. For although in the eyes of the rest of the family she was being absurdly soft over Kevin, the burden of what she had had to say to him had been bitter, vituperative – and hopeless.

It was true and he knew it. He hated everything and everybody, not least on the horizon himself. As he crossed the garden at the beginning of his targetless bid to escape, he hated the garden – hated it for its memories of infant discipline and adolescent frustration. He hated the garden next door, which he had to cross – because he hated the people next door – because they hated him – for the same

137

reason that he hated everybody else – because everybody had got hold of the wrong end of every stick.

He did not know where he was going. He had practically no money on him: Bootsie had wormed her way into handling what she called the privy purse when they were together. Were they ever going to get together again? He thought of going to Steve's, but there was the unbearable thought that this time the magic of Steve's was unlikely to work. Because what he had done at the Cottage Hospital had been unpardonable in any man's code. In panic when the kid had run for it, he had abandoned Bootsie, had left her even without wheels.

He came out on the Bagshawe ring-road. In the car-park of a trendy out-of-town pub he found a Volkswagen Beetle carelessly unlocked. He did not carry a comprehensive ring of car keys, but he had a few and miraculously one that worked on the VW. He drove off: towards Steve's. He could think of nowhere else to go.

Bootsie was wondering why, after initially stalling, she had let Len Saunders get her in tow again. Because she needed a man? No; she could not stand Saunders's style. Because she needed a strong arm if things got rough? No; when it dawned on Saunders who she was and the trouble that she stank of, she knew she wouldn't see his dust. For the sake of mobility, then? That was more like it. She needed to be able to get about. And riding on the back of a more or less anonymous Yamaha was good first-line cover: she thought.

She realized too that it wasn't going to help matters, being unable to produce Janet Morrison – especially if it came to a lone encounter with Miley. Where the hell was the kid? In a moment of feeble optimism she tried to make herself believe that all she'd done was cut and run: could even now be sipping a hot milky night-night drink at home, before her father pissed the fire out.

Don't kid yourself, Bootsie. You know bloody well what she's done. The little bitch!

Saunders rode on full throttle, heading inevitably for Steve's. When she saw the graffiti, the helmets spread about the tables, the ketchup crusted on the spouts of plastic dispensers shaped like garish tomatoes, she was reminded of a line of Housman's:

Then on my tongue the taste is sour of all I ever did.

'Oh, Christ – it's Miley!'

Hatless as always, his almost bald head close-cropped, brawny arms swinging angrily, no jacket, despite the chill of the night, his shirt open at the neck and for two buttons down, a chest like a bullock's – Miley was striding it out from Penscar Wood to Comstock Fiveways, still carrying Sergeant Harman's false packet. Emily Morrison sank back into the passenger seat of Ben Eagle's old banger.

'Do you think he saw us?'

'Couldn't have,' Ben Eagle said. 'You can't see people in cars at night.'

'But he'll know this car.'

'Not him. You can't even see the colour of a car in this light.'

Miley's wife held her peace – not because she was persuaded, but because all her life she had always known when she had said enough.

If Miley knew! If he knew that she had begged a lift from one of his friends! If he knew she was alone with a man in a car under cover of darkness! If he knew what she had done – !

She had drawn £500 from the building society account, that Miley did not know about. She had been out to Penscar Wood earlier than the time ordered in the ransom note. Because she had no room for bringing the police into this. She did not trust them – and who would tell what the kidnappers might do to her Janet, if they found out about this duplicity?

If she could get there first, she argued that she might be able to deposit the payment in time to get Janet back before there was a payoff for treachery –

She had got there first. She had found the yellow stone and a note from Bootsie under it. She put her money down and replaced the stone. The kidnappers had changed their rendezvous. Janet would be handed over in Redfern's barn. Emily Morrison was on her way there now.

Thank God her husband was walking in the opposite direction!

Grimshaw asked himself for the thirtieth time whether his radio silence had been such a good idea. At the moment of decision it had seemed the obvious only choice. After all, Penscar Wood and the Fiveways Crossroads were negotiable places, and he had five hundred men out on the ground against two of them.

What his imagination had failed to deliver to him was a picture of what it would be like in a dark (and cold) car, with only the monotonous breathing of his driver for company, completely out of touch with anything that was going on.

He had sent scouts out to get reports from his outposts. The man he had sent to Penscar had not returned yet, but he now knew that Emily Morrison and Ben Eagle were unaccountably driving about the countryside. He knew that Miley was heading on foot for Fiveways. And he himself had safely followed Bootsie and Saunders and seen them go into Steve's. Twenty minutes later he had seen a Volkswagen Beetle arrive and watched Kevin Toplady enter the cafe. Grimshaw parked behind a stack of oil-drums in the farthest corner of the waste ground outside Steve's and kept watch. There were many things he would have ordered differently if he could have the chance to make up his clipboard for the evening afresh, but there was one principle to which he remained firm: there was to be no move on the part of any of his men until he was absolutely certain that the girl was in no danger.

But where was she? Had they got her in the café, perhaps hidden away in one of Steve's back rooms? If that was the case, then sooner rather than later they were bound to bring her out.

Then another car drove up. Grimshaw wiped vapour from the window and peered out. There was no mistaking the identity of the two men who got out of it: Mosley and Beamish.

Beamish locked the car doors and tested their handles. Then unhurriedly, and with no effort at concealment, they walked in where for the moment even Grimshaw feared to tread.

Eighteen

When Mosley and Beamish went into Steve's there were eight motor-cyclists sprawled round a table covered with bright red grease-spattered plastic. Kevin Toplady was sitting apart from anyone else, looking morose and friendless. He had a cup of tea and a bacon sandwich that had cost him every last penny he possessed.

Bootsie and Len Saunders were alone at one of the other tables. A plate of egg and chips had just been put in front of Saunders. Bootsie was not eating. The atmosphere was a permanent blend of cigarette smoke and deep-frying.

There was a stir among the main body of riders when the detectives came in. They were an out-of-town bunch who did not know Mosley by name or reputation, but who recognized the pair as policemen. They struck up loud conversations intended to convey trite, absurd insults – remarks about curious smells and beating up demonstrators. When Mosley and Beamish tried to walk the length of the room to reach Bootsie, outstretched legs obstructed their progress, and there was no spontaneous effort to move them. Kevin was looking white-faced and frightened. Saunders looked superciliously amused when he saw that he and Bootsie were the immediate target. Behind his counter Steve himself, a sick-looking, fleshless, middle-aged man, was obviously ready with a torrent of disclaimers.

Mosley and Beamish pushed their way past the riding-boots and clutter. Chairs were scraped along the floor so that it would be even more difficult for them to come away.

'Can I get you anything, Inspector?'

Steve brought out Mosley's rank in case anyone was in doubt.

'No, thank you. We shan't be here long.'

He looked at Bootsie.

'Where is she?'

'I don't know what you're talking about,' Saunders said.

'Then keep out of it,' Mosley told him, in a tone that not many people had ever heard him use. 'Unless you badly want to get in on this. Where is she?' he repeated to Bootsie.

'Where's who?' Bootsie asked.

For a moment Mosley looked at her with pity for her meagre intelligence.

'You'll have to do better than that,' he said at last. 'I don't know how long you think you can make that line spin out.'

'Don't tell him anything,' Saunders advised her.

Mosley twisted his torso to look squarely at him.

'I'm still not sure at the moment how deep you are in this, but if you want to dig a little hole for yourself you're welcome. It isn't twopenny ha'penny charges that are going to come out of this, my lad. And if any harm's come to that child, I don't have to tell you what sort of sentences are going to be handed out.'

'I've had nothing to do with any of this.'

'Frankly, you've been puzzling me,' Mosley said. 'Frankly, I haven't been able to fit you in. Till now. Something's just occurred to me. I think I've got the measure of you now.'

Two men came up to the counter and lurched deliberately against Mosley's table as they passed.

'Miss Bateman wouldn't have dared to come into Bagshawe Broome,' Mosley said. 'So somebody must have delivered the vital message. There's a question of a note pegged to a clothes-line. Let's put that down to you, shall we, Saunders? That should see you home.'

The two who had come to have their tea mugs refilled were now breathing over Mosley's shoulders. He got up and thumped the table with a spoon.

'Out there there's the biggest concentration of my friends these hills have ever seen. I'm going to send Sergeant

143

Beamish to get a team together, and we'll have them do spot-checks on any of your bikes that are still on these premises ten minutes from now: brakes, tyres, insurance –'

No one moved – but the volume of their voices diminished noticeably.

'Sergeant Beamish –'

There was a not very hearty ironic cheer as Beamish picked his way through the impedimenta. Mosley sat down again and turned to Bootsie.

'Where is she? Would you like me to closet you with her father for a few minutes?'

Bootsie looked at him as if she were assessing many issues at once. She must surely know that the irresponsibilities of the last two years ended here: there was a strong-willed, prosaic air of finality about Mosley.

'Don't you feel relieved that this is all over?' he asked her.

She closed her eyes for several seconds, then spoke wearily.

'I don't know where she is – but no harm will have come to her.'

'What makes you so sure of that?'

'She can look after herself, can that one.'

'I'm afraid that's not a safe assumption. At least, it's one that I daren't make. When did you last see her?'

'This afternoon.'

'At Waterbrigg Hall?'

'That's right.'

'She slipped your guard? In that case, why hasn't she arrived home?'

'She'll be in no hurry to get home – any more than the rest of us are.'

'Don't talk in spirals. What are you trying to say?'

'Janet Morrison slipped off because she'd decided to go it alone.'

'Go what alone?'

'Get the ransom money.'

Three or four of the motor-cyclists got up in leisurely fashion and started picking up their gear, making it clear that they had not sunk to instant co-operation. Within three minutes, every one of them had left. Kevin Toplady also got up and started sidling with the pack towards the door. But Beamish was returning through it and pushed him back with the flat of his hand against his chest.

'Bring him over here,' Mosley said.

Kevin came and sat at the table, keeping his distance from Bootsie – and his eyes off her.

'I'm arresting you three,' Mosley said. 'We'll go into the details in the charge-room. For two of you thefts from Soulbury Manor will be on the bill of fare, also Lytham St Anne's, Henry Burgess's Garth – and a share of Janet Morrison for all three of you.'

'I want my solicitor,' Kevin said.

'Have you ever met one?'

'I'm saying nothing.'

'Your privilege. I should have cautioned you, shouldn't I?'

He did so now, patiently and clearly.

'I've had nothing to do with –'

'I know. You've had nothing to do with Janet Morrison since you so gallantly ran for it from the Cottage Hospital. I suppose you think that stands to your credit. And Saunders – you can't escape that note on the clothes-line.'

'I'd no idea what was in it.'

'Write that down, Sergeant Beamish. We'll count it as a confession.'

Mosley breathed in and out deeply, but it was not a sigh.

'What do you think we shall get?' Bootsie asked him.

'I wouldn't like to try to guess. It will partly depend on the judge's ulcers. There are some things the courts don't like at all: kidnapping children is one of them. Criminal damage in other people's houses is another. It will also depend on what hope they see for you. You could get a suspended sentence – or you could go down for a stiffish spell. But I'll tell you one thing: sooner or later you'll find yourself in the machine – social workers, probation officers, trick-cyclists, after-care. Make the most of them. They vary – but they have been known to help. I can quite imagine you'll shine in group therapy sessions. You might even end up a social worker yourself. I've known funnier things happen.'

Grimshaw fumed. This time it was going to be a disciplinary panel for Mosley – and if a once-promising sergeant like Beamish had no more sense than to get himself embroiled to this extent, that had to be his own look-out. Grimshaw could not remember that a detective-inspector had been disciplined while he had been in the Force, but there was going to be no backing away from it this time. He made a note to set this in train tomorrow morning. It went on his clipboard, so it was as good as done.

He was aghast at Mosley's nerve – at the man's *thickness*. By rushing in as he had, he had wrecked the evening's operation. Should he himself go into the café now and do his best to sweep up whatever had been shattered? He was irresolute: it needed thinking out carefully.

Then Beamish came out with firm steps, holding his back straight. He walked out of sight behind the far flank of the squalid hutment. What on earth could he want to be doing there? Grimshaw came out of his car intending to follow Beamish and confront him. But Beamish was not away for long. He came back and opened the café door again. As he did so, a crowd of motor-cyclists swarmed out, and Grimshaw saw that Kevin Toplady was also trying to shove his way through. Beamish pushed him back in again with the palm of his hand. And that was another thing. That amounted to technical assault – in front of all those young hoodlums! It was the sort of incident the Force was never allowed to hear the last of.

There was an intolerable racket as eight motor-cycles started up. They rode away with their engines revving full blast. Any hope Grimshaw might have had of listening at the door or windows of the café was stillborn. He had to go in, to retrieve anything that could be retrieved of his strategy.

At a table in the far depths of the café, Mosley appeared to be holding out at length for the Bateman girl's benefit. Grimshaw stood and listened. What the blazes did Mosley think he was now – an Old Testament prophet?

Mosley finished his homily, got up and came towards Grimshaw, smiling in a manner that was meant to be either disarming or insolent.

'These three are under arrest.'

'You've arrested them?'

Grimshaw wondered if there was any way – deep breathing, or something like that – by which he could keep his blood pressure under reasonable control. He was beginning to feel the pulse behind his retinas.

'You told me, with Sergeant Beamish, to clear up once and for all these thefts from unoccupied premises.'

'Thefts! Pettifogging thefts! Candlesticks! A tarnished old sword! China dogs –!'

'No, sir, I think you're forgetting. The china dogs were –'

Grimshaw could see silver flashes.

'Never mind about the bloody china dogs, Mosley. Where's the child?'

'They don't know, sir.'

'Have you made a thorough search of this place?'

'No, sir. Waste of time. She's not here.'

'How can you say that if you haven't looked?'

They had to look now. Beamish had to be left on guard while Grimshaw and Mosley went over the kitchen, the storerooms and the dingy private quarters. Steve made no difficulty: he was only too anxious to show himself in the clear.

Then they had to do the garage and outhouses: dirty, stinking and cluttered with junk.

'We'll have to call up a squad to turn every stick of this over, Mosley.'

'You won't find her,' Mosley said.

'If you're so damned sure of that, where is she?'

'That I don't know for certain. Have you the OS sheet in your car, sir?'

'Of course. Why? Do you think her whereabouts are likely to be marked on the map?'

'I just want to check on something.'

Mosley studied the sheet under a pencil-torch, made dividers of a finger and thumb to measure distances.

'Yes. That'll be it. That's where she'll be. Upper Akehurst.'

Upper Akehurst was a joke village, remote even by the standards of this place.

'Why Upper Akehurst?'

'I'm just trying to put myself into the child's mind, sir.'

'Do you think you might try a little direct communication with my mind, Mosley?'

'Sarah Wainwright lives in Upper Akehurst.'

'Sarah Wainwright?'

'Janet Morrison's bosom friend. The one she was sitting doing quadratic equations with on Bradburn bus-station when she was picked up by Miss Bateman.'

'And?'

'I've just been checking on distances. We are seven miles from Bagshawe Broome and Janet has already had an active evening. She has walked from Waterbrigg Hall to Penscar Wood. That's three miles, so she wouldn't really care to walk back to Bagshawe. She wouldn't want to go there anyway. Upper Akehurst is four miles from Penscar: that, I think, would be within her capacity.'

'There are police cars on the move all over the place, Mosley. All she'd have to do would be to raise a hand.'

'With respect,' Moseley said. 'She'll have been giving any of us a very wide berth.'

'Why should she?'

'Because of what she'll be carrying. She'll go to her friend's. She could be there already. Perhaps there's a report in at HQ.'

Grimshaw broke his wireless ban at last, but neither Upper Akehurst nor the Wainwrights had been heard of at his rear HQ. He therefore sent Beamish back to HQ with two aides to help him with Bootsie, Kevin and Saunders. Grimshaw had decided that now Mosley had nicked them, they might as well stay nicked.

He and Mosley drove, slowly, peering into every shadow, up to Upper Akehurst. The night was frosty, not a shred of cloud to obscure the stars. Here and there a patrol car was parked in a gateway. Grimshaw stopped to tick off an officer whose glowing cigarette he had spotted from seventy-five yards.

They came to Upper Akehurst, a hamlet strung up a winding hill. The Wainwrights' house was in darkness. If ever door, windows and chimneys symbolized honest sleep within, this was the classical case.

148

'Well, Mosley?'

'Clearly she hasn't arrived yet. I suggest we knock the Wainwrights up, then they'll be ready. They're bound to brew us a pot of tea – they'll need one themselves.'

'Mosley – we can't possibly –'

But Mosley was already working on the door knocker, with a vigour likely to conscript the whole of Akehurst to the reception committee. Molly Wainwright turned out to be a jolly but worried woman. Ted Wainwright was a perpetually worried man. And no – they had had no word from Janet. They were surprised that Mr Grimshaw would think they might have done. It was true the girls were school-friends, and Janet had been here once or twice. But –

Mosley looked at his watch.

'Perhaps we've miscalculated. Let's give it another half-hour.'

'If she were on the road, we'd have passed her on the way,' Grimshaw said.

'At the sight of any car on the road, she'd have been over a wall.'

It was two in the morning when Janet Morrison tapped the Wainwright's knocker as discreetly as the Wainwrights' knocker could be tapped. She looked physically tired, sat down with the dramatic gratitude for a chair. She also looked remarkably clean; she seemed to have a capacity for looking clean in the most discouraging circumstances. And mentally she was untarnished.

'My goodness – I must have walked twelve miles tonight!'

Mosley was the only one who was not effusive at the sight of her.

'Don't exaggerate, Janet,' he said. 'It's not been a step more than seven.'

'It's still been a long way,' she said.

She had reverted now to the brand of genteel speech she reserved for impressing her teachers.

'I thought I'd better come here, and if you wouldn't mind ringing people for me, Mrs Wainwright –'

Molly Wainwright lavished hugging affection on her, produced soup and the assurance of a bed. Her own daughter came down the stairs, rubbing her eyes, slow to understand what was happening.

'Did I see you carrying a small bundle as you came through the gate?' Mosley asked, when the child had been installed at the kitchen table. 'Where is it, Janet? Hidden up your jumper? See what she's got under her jumper, Mrs Wainwright.'

Grimshaw was a man of mixed potential and he knew from chastened experience the signs that Mosley was about to deliver the goods. Janet's natural reaction was to back away, but Mrs Wainwright did not miss the significance of that. She gave Janet short shrift, and brought out a packet done up in brown paper.

'You must be adept at dodging about woods and fields at night, Janet,' Grimshaw said, trying to keep the conversation pleasant while Mosley was fumbling with the wrapper.

'I'm a Girl Guide. We camp sometimes in Penscar Wood, and play wide games round here.'

'I'm afraid you're not going to find that parcel's worth much,' Grimshaw said. 'It's only a mock-up.'

But it was found to be a bundle of a hundred used five-pound notes. Janet explained with sweetness and simplicity.

'You see, I knew that my mother wouldn't let me down, whatever my father did or didn't do. I suppose I was taking a chance. But I got there first and got the money back.'

'You really are a most remarkable girl for your age,' Grimshaw told her.

Mosley said nothing.

'In all the circumstances,' Grimshaw seemed to be finding it difficult to look Mosley in the eye this morning – 'And bearing in mind what we achieved last night, we'll say *All's Well that Ends Well*. But this is the last time, Mr Mosley.'

Mosley appeared to hold no opinion on the subject.

'Of course,' Grimshaw said, 'Toplady and Saunders are simply mindless. They're not worth a week's gruel to the exchequer. But I should like to see the girl get a stiff handout.'

'I wouldn't, sir.'

'Explain your thinking, Mosley.'

'I think you heard what I told her last night – about the machine.'

'You have more confidence in the machine than I have. At least you'll agree with me that the child is truly remarkable.'

'True,' Mosley said, but he meant the opposite of what Grimshaw did, and he made it look like that. 'So remarkable that I can see her in real danger if we don't get her into the machine herself soon.'

Emily Morrison got her money back without her husband being told the part that she had played. Detective-Superintendent Grimshaw connived at this out of the goodness of his heart. Her daughter Janet also connived. That cost her mother ten of the five-pound notes.

Beamish solved single-handed the mystery of Veronique's Boutique. It seemed that Bessie Bullough's young ladies were all personable and all hard workers. They were also consummate needlewomen too. Their forte lay in making near-copies of new fashions that Bessie and they had seen in catalogues and at shows, and that she was able to sell at midway prices between the originals and cheaper, later imitations.

Beamish did climb illicitly into the rear of the premises, but was able to gain no vantage point from which he could see anything but personable young women at their machines. He was therefore driven *in extremis* to going in one evening through the front door, as if he were just another of the endless stream of male visitors.

'Ah,' Bessie said. 'You want to join our little club? I've seen you taking an interest in us from across the road.'

She showed him into a capacious basement under her workroom, and there the biggest model railway he had ever seen was being operated to a complex schedule by bank managers, Rotarians, accountants, lawyers' clerks, architects and insurance brokers. Sometimes, he learned, it was

necessary for members to go in during the daytime, to deal
with elusive blown fuses, burned-out circuits and signal
failures.

Kevin Toplady was remanded on bail on his father's recog-
nizances. One of the conditions was that he should make
no attempt to contact Elizabeth Bateman. His mother
bought another tin of salmon for their first high tea together
as a family. If there is anything that Kevin Toplady cannot
stand, it is tinned salmon. It reminds him excruciatingly
of the unutterable misery of Sunday tea when he was
a boy.

It is Saturday morning on Bagshawe Broome Market.

Miley's spot is not available to him on Market Day. He
has to do the best he can from a point on the pavement from
which he can see much, but not everything. Mosley allows
himself to be more mobile.

For old time's sake he goes to cast a friendly eye over
Dickie Holgate's stall, watches a woman buy a leather
umbrella case from the 1920s. Another is asking the price of
a pair of shepherd's dagging shears. Two others are on the
brink of falling out over a banjolele that neither of them will
ever learn to play. When there is a lull in trade, Dickie
beckons Mosley.

'You do operate a small fund to reward informants, Mr
Mosley?'

Mosley is non-committal.

'I'm out of pocket over something I just bought – but I
thought I'd better keep the evidence among friends.'

It is a collectors' limited edition of the *Decameron* in a
tooled leather binding.

'The name on the fly-leaf is Hamble-Petheridge,' Holgate
says. 'That's Waterbrigg Hall.'

'Who sold you this?'

'Miley.'

'I'll give you a receipt for it. I was damned certain
she hid something in the garden before she came to the

152

Wainwrights' door. This is her ticket into the machine, Dickie. *Whack-ho!*

Ten minutes later, Mosley sees Janet out shopping with her mother.

'I'd like a little word with you,' he says.

'What, me, Mr Mosley?'

About the Author

John Greenwood/John Buxton Hilton is the author of the Inspector Kenworthy novels under his own name, and has been a published writer for several decades. Until his death, he lived in Norwich, England, with his wife, Rebecca.